AGED FOR MURDER

AGED FOR MURDER

(A Tuscan Vineyard Cozy Mystery—Book 1)

FIONA GRACE

FIONA GRACE

Debut author Fiona Grace is author of the LACEY DOYLE COZY MYSTERY series which includes MURDER IN THE MANOR (Book #1), DEATH AND A DOG (Book #2), CRIME IN THE CAFE (Book #3), VEXED ON A VISIT (Book #4), and KILLED WITH A KISS (Book #5). Fiona is also the author of the TUSCAN VINEYARD COZY MYSTERY series.

MURDER IN THE MANOR (A Lacey Doyle Cozy Mystery—Book #1) is available as a free download on Amazon!

Fiona would love to hear from you, so please visit www.fionagraceauthor. com to receive free ebooks, hear the latest news, and stay in touch.

TABLE OF CONTENTS

CHAPTER ONE

Olivia Glass had exactly five and a half minutes to manage an unexpected disaster.

It was seven-thirty p.m. on a Thursday night, and she was in the back of an Uber, on the way to meet her boyfriend, Matthew, for dinner at one of Chicago's hottest new restaurants. He'd been out of town all week and had messaged her that morning with the invite.

Now she had discovered a massive rip in her pantyhose, just above the knee.

Olivia stared in horror.

The hole in the black nylon was enormous. It was at least two inches across, and was starting to run up her leg.

She had no idea when this could have happened. The pantyhose had been perfect this morning when she'd put them on. Since seven a.m. she'd been in her office at JCreative, the advertising agency where she worked as an account manager, spending most of the day in meetings and teleconferences.

After receiving the surprise invite to the trendy Villa 49 from Matt, she'd realized that she wouldn't have time to go home and change, and had rushed to the shops during the only free half-hour she had. Panicking because she was running out of time, she'd grabbed something off the rack that was shorter and clingier than she usually wore.

Back at the office, buyer's remorse had descended, and she'd started to wonder if the dress wasn't too daring for a thirty-four-year-old woman to wear.

"Age is but a number," she'd told herself bravely. So what if the dress had been designed for an eighteen-year-old? Although she was a little heavier now, it wasn't as if she'd been a stranger to the gym since then.

As soon as her boss, James Clark, the owner of JCreative, had left the building, Olivia had changed in the restroom at work. She'd run her fingers through her shoulder-length blonde hair, refreshed her lipstick, sprayed on some perfume, and rushed downstairs to meet her ride.

She hadn't realized until she saw the damaged pantyhose how pale her legs were. Even though it was the middle of June, she'd been working so hard they hadn't had a chance to see any summer sun. Through the rip, which Olivia now estimated was about the size of a dinner plate, her skin was blindingly white.

Matt would notice, Olivia knew for sure. He would spot the rip immediately. He was very detail-oriented, which was what made him a highly successful and wealthy investment fund manager. Even though they'd been together for four years, Olivia always tried to look her best for him and make him proud. Her pantyhose disaster would be a publicly embarrassing moment for both of them; the stuff of nightmares.

She had difficult things to confess to Matt during this meal. A wardrobe malfunction would complicate the situation.

For a moment, she considered taking her pantyhose off and arriving bare-legged. She could wriggle out of them in the back of the Uber, and hope that the driver didn't realize what was happening and give her a one-star rating for using his vehicle as a change room.

She shook her head. Pantyhose removal was not an option. Her legs were positively blue-white, and she already felt self-conscious that this dress was shorter than her usual attire. She needed all the help the black nylon hose could give her.

Briefly, Olivia considered ripping an identical hole in the other leg, before deciding that this was impractical. There was no guarantee it would tear the same way, and in any case, she couldn't carry it off. She didn't even feel comfortable wearing ripped jeans.

What to do? The hole was roughly the size of a small car, her destination was now three minutes away, and she had no solutions to her crisis whatsoever.

Then Olivia saw her salvation ahead.

Beyond the next intersection she spotted the signboard for a lingerie and hosiery boutique that looked to be open.

She would ask the driver to drop her there, rush inside, change into a new pair as fast as she could, and call another Uber to take her the rest of the way. She'd be a few minutes late, but at least she'd arrive with a full and undamaged set of clothing.

"Could you please—" Olivia began.

Then her cell phone rang.

Reflexively, she grabbed the call and found herself speaking with James.

"Olivia. Are you still in the office?"

"I've just left. Is it urgent? I can check my email immediately."

Olivia found herself sitting straighter, and she could hear the bright, brisk, professional tone that she instinctively adopted when conversing with her boss.

"Not urgent, but important. We need to meet first thing tomorrow. In the meantime I've had some more great feedback on the Valley Wines campaign."

Olivia felt her heart sink as the Uber accelerated past the boutique. Her only chance had gone. Now they were heading into West Loop, the area characterized by its juxtaposition of old and new—low brick buildings and glass-clad skyscrapers, fine restaurants lining the streets, and a notable absence of any underwear stores.

She was going to arrive at Villa 49 in precisely two minutes with a hole in her pantyhose the size of the International Space Station, and there was nothing she could do about it.

"I'm glad the campaign's going well," she said.

"I'll be sending you an email later, with details about your bonus. You're going to do extremely well out of this."

The cab swerved to pass a bus, and Olivia's purse tipped onto its side. The contents fell out and scattered over the seat.

"You know who Des Whiteley is?" James continued.

"I think I've seen him copied on emails," Olivia said, making a desperate grab for her perfume atomizer as the cab zigzagged again.

"He's the CEO. The chief executive officer."

"Of Valley Wines?" she asked.

"No, no. Of their holding company, Kansas Foods. He asked me to pass on his personal congratulations to you. Sales are through the roof."

"That's amazing." Olivia stretched over to reach her wallet, her lipstick, and a rogue Kleenex.

Her eyeshadow, the small compact she always carried with her, was under the Kleenex.

The color was Shimmering Charcoal.

It gave Olivia an idea.

She opened the box and rubbed her finger over the eyeshadow. Then she rubbed it over her exposed leg.

Success. Shimmering Charcoal turned her skin pantyhose-colored. It camouflaged the damage so that it was almost undetectable.

"I told him that your approach to this campaign epitomized our company's values," James continued. "Methodical and organized."

"Organized," Olivia repeated, scooping up another finger full of eyeshadow.

"Creatively disciplined and results-oriented."

"Results-oriented," Olivia echoed in agreement, rubbing the charcoal powder into the gap.

"Planning for every eventuality," James said.

"Absolutely. Planning."

She should color in a wider area, Olivia decided, as the pantyhose might shift when she walked, or the run might travel higher. Carefully, she eased her finger under the nylon.

"We'll speak tomorrow. I'll be in the office at seven a.m., so let's start then. We'll need at least two hours set aside. We'll have a short one-on-one briefing, and then a group meeting in the boardroom."

What could it be about? Olivia wondered.

"I'll see you there," she said, and he disconnected.

Olivia closed the compact and put it back in her bag.

The success of the campaign had surprised everyone, herself included. As the only woman on the senior executive team, despite her years of hard work, she'd been used to applauding while others' achievements were lauded. She'd never thought it would be her turn to head up a runaway success. In a way, this campaign had felt a lot like camouflaging the damage to her pantyhose.

She felt as if she'd gotten lucky while winging it, and didn't really deserve it, or even want it at all.

"You said something?" The Uber driver interrupted her thoughts, glancing back at her. "You were going to ask me a question, then your phone rang."

"Oh. No, it's all right now. I thought I needed to stop earlier, but it turns out I didn't."

He nodded. "You mentioned Valley Wines. You work for them?"

"Not directly," Olivia said. "I work for an agency that handles their account."

"Are they any good? My wife likes one of the California brands. I can never remember the name, but it's got a pretty label. We haven't been able to find it recently so I told her she should try another."

Olivia felt a stab of guilt. Shelf space was limited, and the gains made by Valley Wines meant other brands had lost out.

For a moment, she considered giving a standard response that the wines were great, and his wife must definitely try them. Then she decided not to. After all, she and the Uber driver were strangers, and it was always easier to be honest with strangers.

"My personal opinion?" she said. "Don't touch Valley Wines. They're horrible, cheaply made, and not worth the money."

They had arrived. The cab stopped outside Villa 49.

"Thanks for the advice," the driver said. "We'll look for a different wine."

"You're welcome. Thank you for the ride." Olivia climbed out.

With her wardrobe disaster under control, it was time to think about what she wanted to say to Matt.

"I'm sure this will come as a shock to you, but I'm really unhappy."

That was going to be her starting point.

Mulling over what she should say next, Olivia walked into the restaurant.

Chapter Two

Olivia stood for a moment inside Villa 49, taking in the subdued lighting, listening to the murmur of voices, and breathing in the aromas that wafted toward her from a table nearby.

The fragrant notes of roasted garlic, thyme, rosemary. The rich aroma of gravy, laced with a mellow hint of wine. The mouthwatering scent of crusty bread, fresh from the oven.

For the first time in the long, stressful day, she felt truly contented. If she closed her eyes, she could imagine herself standing under an olive tree in a rustic trattoria in Tuscany itself, far away from the pressure of her job and the back-to-back meetings and the constant pinging of her phone.

She could even forget about the sensitive conversation she was going to have with Matt.

"Good evening, signora. Welcome to Villa 49. Do you have a reservation?"

The maître d's polite welcome brought her back to reality.

"Yes, it should be in the name of Matthew Glenn."

"Follow me."

She weaved her way through the restaurant behind him.

The corner table that Matt had reserved was empty. Olivia was momentarily surprised. He was always punctual, and she'd arrived five minutes late. She'd expected him to be there, waiting for her.

All the same, traffic could be unpredictable.

Quickly, she checked her phone. There were two more messages of congratulations from her colleagues. Each gave her an identical pang of guilt. Finally, there was a message from her assistant, Bianca.

"James said I have to attend an urgent meeting tomorrow. Do you know what that's about? Have I done anything wrong?"

Olivia could imagine the slim young woman biting her nails in anxiety as she waited. Olivia had tried her best to help her assistant break this nervous habit. She'd even treated her to a manicure, but Bianca had bitten her freshly painted nails just as badly. Eventually, Olivia had decided to leave it be. After all, there were worse habits than nail biting. One of the other assistants had started eating donuts to relieve her stress, and had gained twenty pounds in three months.

Olivia typed back. "Nothing wrong! It's a group meeting, so probably just an assessment and update."

She added a smiley face and sent the message. Then she turned her attention to the wine list.

Paging through the menu, Olivia felt happy all over again. She loved Italian wines, and this menu specialized in labels from the Tuscan region. Some of them she had never heard of, but she was entranced by the music in their names. Her mind visualized rolling green hills bathed in sunshine, with neat ranks of vines interspersed by clusters of olive trees.

Knowing that Matt preferred drinking red wine, she paid special attention to that side of the menu.

Her eyes were drawn to the Tignanello, described as a rich and full-bodied red, made from the local Sangiovese grapes, redolent with the flavor of black cherries. The price reflected its superb quality, but this was a special occasion and she was sure Matt would be happy to splash out.

She was thrilled that they were finally having dinner together. The past few weeks had been insanely busy for both of them, and Matt had been away almost constantly. It was a standing joke between them that Leigh, his PA who traveled with him, saw more of him than Olivia ever would.

"Hey, Liv. Sorry I'm late."

She looked up to see Matt hurrying toward her through the now full and buzzing restaurant. He was wearing his sharpest charcoal Armani suit, and his dark, graying hair was trimmed to perfection. He was tall, fit, handsome, and super-successful. Even after four years, Olivia couldn't believe they were together.

She would never admit it to anyone, but she sometimes felt a twinge of insecurity when she thought about what a catch Matt was. She comforted herself by thinking that this was a positive. After all, it kept her on her toes, conscious of her own image, and striving for greater career success.

"Hello, Matt," she greeted him with a smile. "It's so good to see you. What a surprise you're back in town. I love your haircut."

Standing up, she tugged her clingy dress down over her hips, hoping that he wouldn't notice the camouflage job she'd done on her pantyhose. She was relieved when he kissed her cheek without making any comment, and they sat down.

Olivia ordered the Tignanello, and while they waited for it to arrive, she began the difficult conversation she'd prepared herself for.

"I'm sure this will come as a shock to you, but I'm really unhappy."

Matt's eyebrows shot up.

"Is that so?"

Olivia took a deep breath. Time to unload.

"It's work. Work is the problem."

Matt blinked rapidly, as if he hadn't expected her to say that.

"How do you mean?" he asked carefully.

"I feel as if I've sold my soul. My life's heading off in a tangent I never expected and I—I hate it."

The truth, and the reason she felt as if she'd sold out, was that Valley Wines went against everything she believed in.

The first time Olivia had attended a tasting of Valley Wines, after drinking just two small glasses, she'd woken the next morning with a vicious, pounding headache that had lasted the whole day.

Two small glasses of wine usually didn't have such a toxic effect. Curious to find out exactly what was in these wines, she'd gone digging. It hadn't been easy, but Olivia was patient and persistent and loved the challenge of a puzzle that was difficult to solve. With online research, careful phone calls, and confidential face-to-face meetings, she had discovered the truth.

"I've researched the company, and they're terrible. They're misrepresenting themselves. It's practically fraud, and my marketing campaign is making everyone believe their claims."

Matt frowned.

"But Liv, that's what marketing campaigns are for."

"No!" she protested. "This is different. This isn't just cheap wine, it's junk wine."

"How do you mean?"

"There are no 'family-owned vineyards.' All the grapes are industrially farmed and machine harvested, and they'll use grapes from anywhere. The cheaper, the better. You can't even take a tour of the winery."

"Why's that?" Matt asked.

"Because there isn't one," Olivia confessed. "There's a huge manufacturing plant, and they basically take alcoholic grape juice and doctor it up with loads of powders and flavorants and additives. They've done research on what taste appeals to the majority of people, and the food scientists have created flavor profiles that they match using the additives. That's what Valley White and Valley Red are."

Matt looked dubious as she continued.

"They use loads of sulfites, which is to prolong the shelf life, and also so that every batch tastes the same. I don't know if it's the sulfites or something else in the wine, but drinking it makes me feel awful."

"I still don't see the problem. It's bad wine, but so what? Can't people make up their own minds when they taste it?" Matt asked.

Olivia let out a frustrated sigh.

"The problem is that all the stores are stocking it now, and that means there's less room for other brands. So my campaign is hurting the companies who really care about wine, and who make it properly. I feel like I've done damage to good winemakers who never deserved it."

Olivia cringed as she thought about the success of the now-famous tagline she'd come up with: "Enjoy Today, the Valley Way."

"I made my own personal tagline," she told Matt. "Valley White Will Spoil Your Night and Valley Red Will Hurt Your Head."

She'd expected him to laugh at that, but he didn't.

Perhaps he was finally starting to appreciate the seriousness of her situation.

"Matt, I'm thinking I need to leave," she said. "I can't keep working for a company that represents brands I don't believe in. Who are busy destroying other brands I do believe in. I'm this close to quitting."

She held up her hand with the thumb and finger pressed together.

That was another standing joke between them, but again it didn't get a laugh from Matt.

"I'm afraid I have some bad news, too," he told her.

Olivia stared at him, wide-eyed.

What had happened? Had Matt lost his job? Was one of his parents ill?

Olivia realized there must have been a reason why he'd invited her here. She'd assumed it was to congratulate her, but it had been for his own reasons, and she'd selfishly monopolized the conversation without even asking first.

"Oh, Matt, I'm so sorry. What is it?" she asked.

"I'm sure this will come as a shock to you."

Olivia blinked, confused that Matt had used the exact words she had used. What on earth was wrong?

For a wild moment, she wondered if Matt was as unhappy with his job as she was with hers. Perhaps he'd had enough of being an investment fund manager and wanted a change. Her thoughts raced ahead, imagining how they might make a fresh start together, move to a different city, or even spend a year on an exotic island. What an adventure that would be, allowing them to relax together and enjoy each other's company.

Olivia had never been enthusiastic about marriage and children, and she knew Matt felt the same, but she longed for the simple luxury of being able to spend uninterrupted time with him, without the onslaught of appointments, meetings, and endless working hours that they both had to cope with. On an island, they could do that.

Then reality caught up. Matt loved his job and had never so much as hinted he was unhappy. Plus, he was a city boy who enjoyed the pace of urban life. It couldn't be that, so it must be something else.

"What will be a shock?" she asked, feeling a chill of apprehension.

"This isn't working."

"What do you mean?" Her own voice sounded small and strange.

"Us." He gave her one of his trademark apologetic smiles, with the tight lips and the crinkled eyes and the incline of his head. "We aren't working. I'm so sorry. I wish this could have gone differently. But this is how it is. There's no easy way to say it, but I'm calling it off."

CHAPTER THREE

Olivia stared at Matt in disbelief.

What was he talking about? Was this a cruel practical joke?

She dismissed the thought instantly. Matt wasn't that kind of person. Then again, she hadn't believed he was the kind of person to invite her to dinner at a fancy restaurant and break up with her before the wine had even arrived.

"But—why?" she asked. "Matt, why are you doing this? We've been happy together. Well, I've been happy. I know we haven't seen each other as much as we could have, but that's because we've both been so busy."

He nodded approvingly as if she'd just hit the nail on the head.

"Exactly, Liv. That's exactly the problem. You've summarized it. We're both so busy. We don't see each other more than one or two nights a week." He leaned forward and spoke in a quiet, confidential tone. "More than that, we're different people. I'm a highly organized person. It's difficult living with someone as disorganized as you. You never put the lid back on the toothpaste, and last week, when I opened my briefcase at a meeting, a pair of your panties fell out. It was extremely embarrassing for me. There were twenty international investors there, and having a pink lacy undergarment with the slogan 'Wish You Were Here' land on the boardroom table negatively affected the professional impression I was hoping to make, and which our firm expects."

Olivia thought she heard a stifled giggle. Glancing around, she saw that their conversation had attracted the attention of the three women at the neighboring table, who were now listening avidly.

"And why did that happen, Olivia?" Matt continued. "It is because you insist on taking them off and throwing them onto the bedroom floor, instead of putting them in the laundry basket. This time, a pair landed inside my briefcase.

It could have been disastrous for my career. That's just one example. You haven't been supportive."

Olivia's mouth fell open. What was he talking about? She'd supported him all the way.

"When we moved in together, I cleared out the spare bedroom so that you could have a study, even though you never used it," she said, outraged now. "I repainted the master bedroom in white because you asked me to. I cleared out my cupboards to make space for all your jackets and shirts and shoes. I even gave away my beautiful bookcase so that your massive flat-screen TV could fit in the family room."

Her furniture and her bed had stayed. Matt had said he would sell his. Or, wait. As Olivia was remembering now, he'd said he would give them to Leigh, his PA, as she'd broken up with her boyfriend and was moving into her own place.

Olivia frowned with sudden suspicion. Before she could say anything, Matt continued as if he hadn't heard her at all.

"Like I said, I've been reviewing my life decisions. And Liv, I feel that we want such different things. Yes, you've been happy, but I want someone who'll be there for me. Who can care for me, cook for me, sort out my life."

"I cook for you!" The words came out louder than Olivia had intended.

The waiter, bringing the wine, did a double take as he approached and set the bottle down.

"May I open—" he began hesitantly, but Matt waved him away.

With righteous indignation, Olivia continued.

"Just last week, I made us spaghetti Bolognese. I got up at five a.m. to prepare the sauce and put it in the slow cooker. It smelled so delicious that even the neighbor complimented it when I arrived back from work. And what did you say, Matt? Do you remember what you said when I served it up? You said, 'Well, I sure hope this won't kill me.' You thought that was so funny and I laughed too, but it was hurtful."

"Keep it down, will you?" Matt said with a tight smile, but she could hear the stress in his words.

Olivia blinked. Keep it down? He was telling her not to shout, after delivering a bombshell that had upset her entire life?

"You are sometimes embarrassing." Matt lowered his voice. "Talking loudly in restaurants is something I've pointed out to you in the past. The whole room doesn't want to hear your funny stories."

"Yes, we do," Olivia heard one of the women at the next door table mutter.

"And did you use eyeshadow to conceal that run in your pantyhose? Aren't you worried people might notice? You could easily have kept a spare pair in your purse, and avoided the problem altogether. That's what an organized person would do."

Olivia felt herself turn crimson.

"I didn't notice that," she heard another of the women say. This time, Matt looked around in surprise.

Olivia drew a deep breath.

"What made you think now was a good time to talk about this?" she asked.

"I'm flying out of the country tomorrow. It's a last-minute arrangement. Short notice, I know."

This conversation was becoming so surreal that for a moment, Olivia was certain she was dreaming all of this. She must be having a nightmare, because nothing was making sense.

"Where are you going?"

"I'm going to Bermuda for two weeks." He didn't meet her incredulous gaze as he spoke the words.

"For work?" Again, she saw Matt wince at the volume of her voice.

"It's a work conference, yes."

"Is Leigh going with you?"

The question was reflexive—she hadn't had time to think it through—but she saw his reaction. For a moment, he looked horrified, as if she'd caught him out.

"You and Leigh? Conferences don't last two weeks. This has nothing to do with work. Does it?"

"Please, keep it down," Matt muttered. "Leigh is my PA. Nothing more. She's much younger than me anyway. She's turning thirty on Sunday."

He stopped, clamping his lips together, but too late. Olivia pounced on the information he'd inadvertently disclosed.

"Turning thirty? That's a big birthday. Her gift wouldn't include a vacation to Bermuda, would it?"

Olivia heard a horrified gasp from the next table.

Guilt was written all over his face. Olivia felt appalled. Thirty-five-year-old Matt was only a year older than she was, and back when they had first started dating, she'd worried that he might look for someone younger. Although she'd known she could do nothing about that, she and her hairdresser had conspired to make sure he couldn't possibly look for anyone blonder. Clearly, it hadn't helped.

"You brought me out to this lovely restaurant and the first thing you do is break up with me?"

She felt shocked all over again by the callousness of his actions.

"You did it so that I wouldn't make a fuss, didn't you? You hoped that because this was being done in a fancy restaurant, you'd be able to walk away without me getting mad or causing a scene."

Olivia jumped to her feet, glaring down at him.

"I am mad. I am furious. And I'm going to cause a scene. You've treated me appallingly. How dare you have an affair behind my back, and then try and make me feel inadequate, saying you need someone to take care of you and implying I didn't do that. It's the most manipulative thing I ever heard."

"It's unacceptable," she heard one of the women from the next table say firmly. "You're well rid of someone who cheats on you and insults your cooking and nitpicks your clothing decisions. Never mind the pantyhose problem, which none of us even noticed, I don't think he mentioned your lovely dress. Talk about looking for the faults."

"You're obviously too good for him, and he feels threatened by you," another of them supplied in helpful tones.

"It's like the trash is taking itself out, honey," the third announced.

"Thank you," Olivia told the women.

Glancing around the restaurant, she noticed that there were several nods of agreement from the other patrons following this drama. A young man at a table near the door had taken out his phone and was preparing to film the scene.

Matt, his face brick red, was staring fixedly down at the starched tablecloth.

"I—I didn't mean it that way," he muttered. "Look, shall we go somewhere else and talk this through?"

He looked as if he was hoping the earth, or perhaps the restaurant's granite tiles, would magically open and swallow him up.

As it was, he was going to have to leave Villa 49 and walk past every one of those people. Each one a newly discovered critic of Matt Glenn. He'd be judged every step of the way, and Olivia decided he could make that walk of shame alone.

"I'm leaving," she said in quieter tones. "If you haven't cleared out your stuff from my apartment by ten p.m. tonight, I'm donating whatever's left to charity."

Her gaze fell on the magnificent Tuscan red, which she'd chosen with such care and excitement. Even though she hadn't gotten to experience the food, she was damned if she was going to leave that wine behind.

"This is coming with me." She seized the bottle from the table, clamping her hand around the cool, dark glass. "You'll find it on the bill."

The women at the next table started to applaud.

Picking up her purse, Olivia turned and marched to the door.

CHAPTER FOUR

Outside the restaurant, Olivia called a cab. She was still trembling with outrage, and felt like marching back into the restaurant to give Matt another piece of her mind.

She took a deep breath to settle herself. It would be more sensible to move on and cut him out of her life forever. That meant finding somewhere else to go now, because she'd given Matt a ten p.m. deadline. She couldn't get back to the apartment earlier in case she found him there, packing up his shirts and suits and taking that oversized flat-screen TV down.

She frowned, indecisive. She had friends, of course. Just—not that many of them, especially here in Chicago. Her working hours over the past years hadn't allowed for much socializing, and her two best friends were away on vacation.

She climbed into the cab and found herself giving the driver Bianca's address, as it was the only street name she could think of.

Twenty minutes later, she was tapping hesitantly on her assistant's front door, hoping that she wouldn't consider it an imposition.

"Is everything all right?" Bianca asked, as soon as she saw Olivia standing on her doorstep. She was wearing a pink tracksuit with a blue rabbit on the pocket, and the delicious smell of pizza emanated from the small flat.

She stared at Olivia uncertainly, and Olivia realized the last thing she'd wanted or expected was for her boss to materialize without warning on her doorstep.

Bianca's hand automatically flew to her mouth and Olivia resisted the urge to grab her wrist as she nibbled her thumbnail.

"I didn't know where else to go," Olivia confessed.

"Has something happened?" Bianca asked.

"Matt invited me to dinner and then broke up with me. I remembered your address. I have wine," Olivia added helpfully, as if that might seal the deal.

Bianca gave a horrified gasp.

"Oh, Olivia, that's awful. Come in. Are you OK? You must be in shock. Please sit down. Can I make you some sweet tea? Isn't that what you are supposed to do for shock? Are you feeling cold, or breathing shallowly?"

"I'm fine," Olivia said.

"Have you eaten? I ordered a large pizza because I was going to keep some for breakfast. It's just arrived. There's more than enough for two."

"That's so kind."

Even though she was still seething with anger, Olivia realized that she was starving. She'd skipped lunch in anticipation of the feast she would enjoy at Villa 49.

Even so, she felt like an intruder in Bianca's space. They worked together for twelve hours or more a day, but they'd never really had the chance to become friends, or to discuss anything that wasn't related to the advertising accounts.

She set the wine bottle down next to the pizza box in Bianca's neat kitchen, opened it, and poured them each a large glass, hoping it would set them at ease.

"I ordered this to drink with the meal. It's from Tuscany," she said.

Lifting the glass, she breathed in the bouquet. Rich, full-bodied, and fragrant, the nose was redolent of dark cherries. This was a wine made with passion and care. It was magnificent.

Taking a small sip, she felt the flavor dance on her tongue. It was as if her mouth was aglow.

Olivia felt a moment of regret that she couldn't have enjoyed this wine with the restaurant's fine food—but a rustic pepperoni pizza, heavy on the cheese, was the best second choice she could think of. She transferred it to plates, and they went into the living room, where the AC was keeping the summer evening's heat at bay.

She and Bianca sat opposite each other. They drank the wine in unison. Then they each ate a slice of pizza. The crust was crunchy, and chewing it broke the awkward silence in the apartment.

Before she knew it, Olivia was refilling their glasses, and suddenly the silence didn't feel impenetrable any longer.

"That's a terrible thing to do," Bianca sympathized, looking anxious all over again. "Inviting you to dinner and then breaking up with you."

Olivia nodded. "I discovered that he was seeing his PA on the side."

"What?" Bianca sounded outraged.

"He's going on vacation to Bermuda with her tomorrow. So I'm more relieved than anything. He showed his true colors. He's an inconsiderate cheat. I had a lucky escape." A thought occurred to her. "By the way, do you notice anything strange about my pantyhose?"

Bianca peered down at them.

"What am I supposed to be looking for?" she asked. "That's a beautiful dress."

"Never mind. I was just checking."

Olivia felt a surge of relief that she was no longer in a relationship with a hypercritical man who clearly had X-ray vision.

She took another mouthful of the incredible wine.

"I must be honest with you, I'm unhappy at work."

"Why?" Clasping her hands, Bianca leaned forward.

"I'm feeling burned out. I'm feeling trapped, in a way. Maybe it's just this campaign, but at the moment I'm totally demoralized."

"Because of the long hours?"

"Partly, but also because I'm worried that I've sold myself out."

Just in time, Olivia remembered that she shouldn't share all the details of Valley Wine's manufacturing process with Bianca, because her assistant still had to work on the account. She continued, choosing her words carefully.

"Our accounts are all so mainstream, big corporate entities without soul. My passion doesn't lie there. I want to support the small businesses, and the artisanal brands. I want to be a part of that lifestyle, instead of caught up in a rat race where characterless brands are battling for supremacy, using our agencies as their weapons."

Bianca looked impressed by her outburst. She nodded solemnly and then gave a loud hiccup.

Olivia was impressed herself. She hadn't found the right words, until now, to voice her perspective so eloquently.

"Would you ask to be moved a different account?" Bianca asked.

Olivia sighed. "I don't know if James would let me, because this has been such a success. They may want to do a follow-up. Plus, as one of the biggest agencies, we tend to handle the larger brands. I don't think we have a boutique product in our stable."

"That is a problem," Bianca sympathized.

Olivia wondered for a confused moment how she'd gotten to this point. She was trapped in the rat race. She had to work to afford her expensive apartment, and she needed her expensive apartment because it was close to work. How could she get off this hamster wheel without causing a major accident along the way? she wondered.

"You know, I have this weird dream of an alternative lifestyle," Olivia shared with her assistant.

"Like a hippie? With a campervan?" Bianca hazarded.

"No, different from that." Olivia felt embarrassed to be sharing her dream, because she'd never talked about it. Not even to Matt, which was just as well, or he would probably have poked so many holes in it that it would have sunk long ago.

"Well, tell me. What?" Bianca leaned forward curiously.

"I can't." Olivia felt ashamed to voice her impossible idea.

"Well, now you have to, or I won't be able to sleep tonight for curiosity," Bianca encouraged.

Olivia took a deep breath.

"I love wine." She paused to gather her thoughts. "I'd like to become part of that industry, buying a small vineyard and producing my own wines. I've always imagined myself doing it somewhere in Italy. I haven't thought about the details, but I can't stop visualizing what life would be like, working in a small town or village. How different it would be."

She took another sip of the Italian red.

"Imagine being out in the Tuscan countryside, in wine-growing territory. To feel part of a local community and make friends who live right next door."

"It sounds amazing." Bianca nodded, wide-eyed.

"It can't be that hard to make wine, can it? I mean, I know quite a bit about how it's supposed to taste." Olivia drained her glass.

"I don't think it's that difficult," Bianca agreed. "You grow the grapes, pick them, trample on them, and then you brew them? It doesn't seem complicated." She nodded thoughtfully, staring at her own empty glass.

"I'm glad you think so. You know, I'm thirty-four years old, I'm single again, and I can count my good friends on the fingers of one hand," Olivia confessed. "Even if I'd had a nasty accident involving heavy machinery, I would still be able to count them on that hand. On the rare times we do get together, we hug and say we're so close it's like we saw each other yesterday. But the truth is, we live far apart and as time passes by, we are growing further away from each other."

Bianca looked crestfallen.

"I see what you mean. That's so sad."

"I'm starting to want something more from life." Olivia sighed, draining her glass. "It's a stupid idea, though. It couldn't happen."

"Why not?" Bianca asked. "I think it sounds wonderful. It seems like exactly the change you need. Maybe you should do it. Go there for a vacation, and see if there are any opportunities. At any rate, take the vacation. You deserve it. You haven't taken more than a couple of days off in the past year."

Olivia smiled.

"It's just a dream. Reality is different. But yes, maybe I will book some leave and take a vacation. That sounds like a good idea."

She ate the last slice of pizza and checked the time.

"I can't go home yet," she said. "I gave Matt until ten p.m. to move his belongings out. I'm sure he's there now and I don't want to see him again."

"Let me open another bottle," Bianca suggested. "I think we could use another glass."

"That's a good idea," Olivia said.

But when Bianca brought the fresh glasses through from the kitchen, Olivia stared at the wine in suspicion.

There was something about that watery, bright red color that looked familiar. She smelled it, breathing in a sweetish, artificial aroma that she recognized only too well.

"What is this?" she asked, keeping her tone conversational.

"It's a bottle of Valley Red," Bianca said, sounding nervous. "You don't mind, do you? I know it's not as good as the one we've been drinking, but we got a free case each at the launch."

Looking at her worried face, Olivia decided there were times to stick to her principles and times when it was more important to be kind.

"Free wine is always good wine," she said bravely.

Her head throbbed in anticipation as she raised her glass.

Doing her best not to grimace as she downed the doctored grape juice, Olivia made a promise to herself.

This was the last time she was drinking this factory-produced swill. She resolved that whatever it took, no matter how much she had to beg James or the damage it caused to her career, she was going to refuse to work on the Valley Wines account any longer.

CHAPTER FIVE

The morning sunshine pierced cruelly through Olivia's white bedroom curtains, hammering into her aching skull.

"Valley Red Will Hurt Your Head," she groaned. She sat up carefully, wincing at the pain.

Half a bottle of Tuscany's finest had been chased with a large glass of sulfite-laden, flavor-enhanced, alcoholized grape juice. At least she knew her headache was well earned. And the wine had provided a welcome numbness when she'd arrived back to her half-empty apartment, where the disordered shelves and scuff marks on the carpet were evidence that Matt had done a hasty late-night clean-out of all his belongings.

Well, he was out of her life forever. Goodbye and good riddance.

She shuffled to the bathroom and swallowed down two Advil with a big glass of water. Then she climbed back into bed, hoping they would kick in soon, because even thinking was painful.

To pass the time, Olivia opened her phone and scanned through her social media. She hadn't had time to update her personal account for weeks, or catch up with what her friends were doing.

She scrolled through Instagram, glad to see that one of her colleagues from her previous work had adopted two kittens. Her feed was filled with pictures of the ginger pair, playing with each other, chasing toys, and snoozing.

Another acquaintance had attended a wedding in Hawaii, and Olivia was mesmerized by the colorful photos.

Then her eyes widened as the next picture came into view.

It was a dramatically beautiful Tuscan villa. Olive trees, warm sand-colored stone, with a vista of hills and vineyards beyond. For a moment she felt as if her own imagination had dreamed this photo up.

Then she saw it was on her friend Charlotte's feed.

Charlotte was Olivia's oldest friend. They had been best friends when they were in school. With both of them being only children, they'd pretended that they were each other's sister, or even twins, to people who didn't know them. Over the years, they'd fallen further and further out of touch, because they'd been working in different cities for so long. Olivia remembered now that Charlotte was getting married soon. Perhaps she and her fiancé were out there scouting for wedding venues.

"#VillaVibes," Charlotte had written. "#TuscanSummer #wine #freedom."

Olivia typed a comment.

"Looks amazing!"

To her surprise, a reply pinged up almost immediately.

"Come visit! I'm here on my own and looking for someone to share. It's two-bedroom and rented for the summer!"

"On your own?" Olivia messaged, with a surprised emoji. "What about the wedding?"

"I called it off. #singleisfreedom #livingwellisthebestrevenge," Charlotte sent back with a string of smiley faces.

Olivia stared at the message in shock. What had gone wrong for her friend to make such a drastic decision? She couldn't help feeling a pang of envy, because Charlotte had clearly decided on a change of scenery, and was getting her life back together in an exotic environment.

In the same situation, all Olivia had done was to drink enough wine to make her head explode.

"If only! Maybe next time!" she replied.

She closed her eyes. If she'd made better life choices, she could be sitting on a wrought-iron swing, chatting with Charlotte under an olive tree, overlooking a stone courtyard with a vista of hills and vines beyond. She could almost imagine how the soft breeze would tug at her hair, as she sipped at a cool glass of Chianti.

Charlotte's coping mechanism seemed much more constructive. But then, Charlotte hadn't been in the throes of a massive work campaign like she was.

Olivia remembered her important meeting this morning. Would she have the nerve to do what she'd promised last night, and take some time off, and then tell James she wanted to transfer to a different account?

Now, in the blinding light of day, with an aching head, it seemed ludicrous. She couldn't possibly do such an irresponsible, spur-of-the-moment thing. She'd be letting people down. They'd think badly of her. In any case, James would say no. He'd probably laugh in her face.

Wrenching her attention away from Instagram, Olivia saw to her horror that it was already six a.m.

While she'd wasted time chatting online and dreaming of Tuscany, a message had pinged up on her phone. It was from James.

"Olivia, I need you here by 6.50 a.m. at the latest. We now have the entire executive team of Kansas Foods and Valley Wines attending this meeting. I need to brief you for 10 mins beforehand."

No matter how fast she got out of her apartment, she was going to be late for her important briefing.

Cursing under her breath, Olivia jumped out of bed, grabbing the first business suit she could get her hands on, scrambling into it, and rushing to the bathroom to do her make-up.

As she turned the light on, with a pop, the lightbulb failed.

Olivia swore again. She was hardly ever late. Well, not regularly. But when she was, why did life conspire against her this way?

She applied her make-up in the semi-darkness, making a mental note to check whether the mascara had smudged.

Then, grabbing her purse and her work folders, she sprinted out of the apartment.

As she passed the neighboring apartment, the door opened.

"Hello, stranger. I wanted to talk to you."

It was Len, her neighbor. Long-Winded Len, as she nicknamed him, because he could never end a conversation quickly. He couldn't even start one quickly, if she was honest. Len earned a fortune doing something obscure in IT and was notably eccentric.

Olivia smiled, although she could sense that it was more of a stressed grimace. Of all the days, Long-Winded Len had chosen today to leave his home at the same time she had.

"I'm sorry. I'm very late for work, and—" Olivia began.

Len continued as if he hadn't heard her, patting down his rumpled hair. He looked as if he was still in his pajamas. Len always looked like that, though, so perhaps he only owned pajamas.

"I asked you last year if you'd consider selling your apartment. I'd just like to remind you of the offer because I'm in urgent need of additional space, and there's nowhere else in the city that has this fiber capacity. You know, as well as needing a study for work, I now have a full set of HO model trains, which takes up an entire room, as well as two Z-scale sets, which might be smaller in size, but which require substantial real estate."

"Is that so?" Olivia drew breath to give him a polite refusal, but he continued.

"I also have acquired three additional cats, who need their own playroom. I can't put them in with the trains." He shook his head sorrowfully. "I tried that and it didn't end well. The trains were on the losing side, you might be glad to hear."

"That's a relief," Olivia said.

"I'm prepared to increase my offer."

Olivia felt ready to scream.

"Len, no, I'm really sorry. Sorry for your cats and your trains. And your additional cats. And your new smaller trains. I don't want to sell but I promise, if I change my mind, you'll be the first to know."

Len didn't seem to be listening anymore. Instead, he was looking at her strangely.

"Did you injure yourself? Have you and your boyfriend had a violent disagreement?"

Olivia blinked.

"No. Why?"

"You appear to have a blackened left eye."

"Oh. It's my make-up. Thanks for telling me."

Rubbing her fingers frantically under her eye, Olivia sprinted for the exit door.

Half an hour later, she reached the tall, glass-clad office tower where JCreative occupied the top two floors.

She took the elevator up, willing it to move faster, and broke into a run as soon as her feet hit the carpeted corridor. She burst into James's office at exactly one minute past seven.

"Sorry I'm late," she gasped.

James sat in his director's chair, which Olivia thought was oversized for him. He was looking at her sternly, as if her tardy arrival was a huge disappointment.

Staring at him, Olivia felt a frisson of fear, because she could see herself heading down the same path. This was all he knew—this company was his life. He'd gotten divorced a few years ago and seldom saw his children. Even though it was summer, she realized how pale his skin looked, as if he never got the chance to relax out in the sun, when all his time was spent playing the corporate game in boardrooms.

"Sit down. I have exciting news for you," he told her.

"What is it?" she asked, forcing a smile.

"Kansas Foods, the holding company of Valley Wines, is impressed by the success of this campaign. They're joking that we've put a cork into their opposition."

Olivia stretched her smile wider, wishing that this really was good news.

"It's not actually a joke, in fact. Three competing brands have lost so much shelf space that they will probably go out of business." Now James smiled.

"That's—um." Olivia couldn't bring herself to say the word "good." It was terrible, and she was to blame for it.

"So, as of today, we will be handling the entire corporate account of Kansas Foods," James announced proudly. "That's why the executive teams are already in the boardroom. We're doing the handover this morning, and we'll be signing a five-year contract for all brands. This deal is worth hundreds of millions of dollars."

Olivia felt her smile freeze into place.

"That's great. What an achievement." She wasn't sure how she sounded, but hoped that James didn't suspect how she felt inside.

"Now, you might be wondering what this means for you," James said. He gave a small smile. "Let's hope you don't have too many vacations planned. You're going to be shouldering a substantial workload, because you will head up all the major campaigns. You'll need to hire a few additional staff, and divide your time between here and their head office, which is located in Wichita. I imagine you'll be spending one week here, one week there. It shouldn't be a problem for you. You're not married, are you?"

Olivia bit back a response. Why would her marital status make a difference? Yes, she happened, as of yesterday, to be without a boyfriend, but why did James, a divorced man, assume that being unmarried and single was one and the same for her?

"I'm not," she said coldly.

James looked surprised, as if he'd expected his words to be received with groveling acquiescence.

"You'll receive a promotion to Account Director, a substantial salary increase, and the bonus structure is double what you had previously. So there's a lot of money to be made, my girl. A lot of money to be made." He rubbed his hands together.

Olivia blinked. She thought she'd already made a lot of money. If more was to come, how much would it be? Didn't they say everyone had their price? She was starting to wonder if she did.

"I—" Olivia began, but James didn't pause.

"One of their biggest accounts with us will be Daily Loaf—that's their bread." He clicked keys on his laptop. "Their CEO gave me some details yesterday. It has a shelf life of up to two weeks. Up to two weeks. Can you believe it?"

"Incredible," Olivia said. She was panicking inwardly. She didn't want to advertise bread with a two-week shelf life. She wanted to work with handcrafted, stone-ground loaves, baked in rustic clay ovens.

"The signature flavor is enhanced by a mixture of sucrose and corn syrup, which makes the bread especially delicious," James continued. "I think we can work that into the campaign. Perhaps something like 'Just One More Slice, Cause It's So Nice'? You'll be able to fine-tune it, I'm sure. They have a health version, too. It has ten percent whole wheat flour added, and obviously less sugar."

James glanced at his laptop.

"No, I see the health bread has the same sugar profile. But added whole wheat, of course, that's a big buzzword right now. Daily Loaf has massive potential, and I can't wait to see what you come up with."

Smiling weakly, Olivia was beginning to feel sick.

"It will be great if you can think up a few ideas, slogans, directions off the top of your head so we can impress them in the meeting. I know you're good at winging it." He raised a conspiratorial eyebrow.

Olivia flinched. Did that mean what she thought?

"I've given you a very strong build-up, so the executive team has high expectations. They're expecting the world from you, but I know you'll deliver. Anyway, back to the products. Let me brief you on the sodas—"

Olivia stood up. She was unable to listen to another word. Not even the prospect of the money, the bonus, and the promotion could persuade her otherwise. No matter how much it was.

"It all sounds very exciting," she said. "But it's not for me, I'm afraid."

She couldn't believe the words were coming out of her mouth. James's horrified expression told her that she wasn't the only one. Unable to stop, feeling that it was now or never and she'd already crossed a line, Olivia continued.

"I can't, unfortunately, work with this brand, or any other associated brands, any longer. So, as of now, I'm handing in my resignation. Please accept it verbally."

"What the hell is this?" James spluttered. "You're talking nonsense. This is crazy. You can't just up and leave!"

"I quit," Olivia said firmly.

Taking a deep breath, she stood up and left the room. Behind her she heard James's despairing cry.

"Olivia. Don't go! We need to talk!"

Staying strong, she forced herself to keep walking and not look back.

Outside, in the street, she felt a terrifying sense of freedom. She looked back at the building's dark glass exterior feeling stunned. Her hands were shaking with shock. What had she just done? It had been a moment of madness, but there was no going back.

This was not her workplace and never would be again. She might never set foot inside it for the rest of her life.

Fear and expectation curdled inside her as she opened Instagram and messaged Charlotte again.

"I've changed my mind," she typed. "Is the villa still available?"

Holding her breath, she waited for a reply.

Chapter Six

The pile of clothes on Olivia's bed was growing.

So far, it contained jeans, shorts, T-shirts, casual tops, and smart tops, as well as some long-sleeved tops and a jacket.

She felt breathless with anticipation as she stared at the clothes. In a few short hours she'd be boarding a plane. Tomorrow morning, she would arrive in Tuscany.

"I'm going. I'm actually going. I don't believe it," she said.

This morning she'd woken hungover, stressed, and hating her job. Just two hours later, she'd quit, booked her flight, and was packing for the trip.

OK, so at least she'd had a job this morning. Today marked the first time in twelve years that she was an unemployed woman. But after her two-week holiday in Tuscany, she could look for another job. Two weeks was a long time. It stretched ahead of her, filled with excitement and possibility.

She rummaged in the back of the cupboard for her running pants. It had been a long time since she'd run. Years, in fact. She hated running, but she was sure, in Italy, that she would love it. And she'd need to keep fit, especially since she'd be drinking wine every evening, and eating pasta with creamy sauce. And cheesy, delicious pizza, and crusty bread dipped in olive oil and balsamic vinegar.

Thinking of all that food, Olivia added her yoga pants to the pile. She'd never been a yoga person, and had only bought the pants because she'd thought of attending a class once. But she could do yoga at the villa. She could Google how. She imagined herself balanced elegantly on her hands as the sun rose.

In another ten minutes, her packing was done.

As she wheeled her heavy bag outside and locked the door behind her, she realized that there wasn't anything she was leaving behind. Not even a plant that needed watering. Was it a sign of how empty her life had become?

"There'll be plants at the villa," Olivia told herself optimistically.

"Amore mio," the handsome man whispered, his lips tickling Olivia's hair. "How wonderful you have arrived. Let me take your bag."

Olivia stared up at him, love filling her heart.

Love, and an underlying sense of confusion. Why was she being met by this gorgeous man, who spoke with a strong Italian accent? Was he her boyfriend? How had this happened and what would Matt think about it?

With ease, the tall man swung her heavy suitcase off the trolley and slid his other arm around Olivia's waist. Olivia's doubts faded away as he held her close. It would all work out somehow, she was sure.

"Let me take you home now, beautiful," he murmured.

The crackle of the announcement wrenched Olivia back to wakefulness.

"We are commencing our descent. Please ensure your chairs are in the upright position and fold away your tables."

Olivia struggled upright, disoriented, smiling apologetically at the woman next to her, whose shoulder she'd been sleeping on. For a confused moment she thought she was on a local flight, about to attend a launch. Then, as she remembered where she was, she stared out the window in excitement.

She was about to land in Italy. She'd quit her job and she'd broken up with Matt, and she was heading off for an impulse vacation at a Tuscan villa.

Olivia caught her breath as the tapestry of fields, hills, and forests came into view. She saw small towns, the buildings in colors of sand, beige, and ocher, nestled into the landscape. Was that a vineyard? She peered down, trying to make out what the neat, green rows were, but had to move back after her breath steamed up the glass.

Her dream had been so vivid it had felt like reality. A handsome man had been waiting to meet her. Well, who knew what might happen on this impulse vacation? As the plane touched down, Olivia wondered if she might meet the love of her life in this romantic setting.

As she walked into the crowded Arrivals hall, pulling her heavy bag behind her, she saw a notice with her name on it.

Olivia Glass.

Olivia stared incredulously.

There must be magic at work. Behind the notice board stood a tall, stunningly good-looking man. He was broad-shouldered and tanned, his strong features enhanced by dark designer stubble.

When he saw her, his face lit up and he waved enthusiastically.

Olivia's eyes widened. She waved back, giving him a delighted smile as she weaved her way eagerly toward him.

Her dream had become reality; her holiday had gotten off to a fairytale start. Who could have imagined that the simple act of renting a car would allow her to meet this Italian Adonis?

Had he recognized her from the photo on her international driver's permit? Olivia speculated over the possibilities as she hurried over to him. It must be the driver's permit, she decided, but she could ask him. It would provide a starting point for their conversation as he escorted her to her car.

As she swerved to avoid a slower moving passenger, Olivia's heavy suitcase tipped onto its side.

"Oops," she said, stopping to right it.

As she did, a petite woman in a stylish, bright red coat brushed past her.

The handsome man was still waving, but Olivia now saw in horror, not at her.

The petite woman reached him and he enfolded her in his arms, hugging her tightly.

Olivia gasped, blushing in mortification as she realized the notice board didn't belong to him at all. It was being held by a short, elderly man standing to his left, who had lifted the board high so that she'd be sure to see it.

Olivia knew her face was turning as crimson as the petite woman's coat.

Worst of all, the Italian Adonis had clearly picked up on her faux pas, because now he was giving her an apologetic, pitying headshake, and a few other onlookers were staring curiously at her, too.

There was only one thing Olivia could do to retrieve the tattered fragments of her dignity.

Ignoring the Adonis as if she'd never noticed him at all, she looked directly at the elderly man. She forced another smile, even bigger than before, and waved again with all her might.

"Hello! It's so good to see you!"

She must not look around, Olivia reminded herself. If her desperate attempt at avoiding lifelong embarrassment was to succeed, she must focus all her attention on the elderly man without so much as a sideways glance at anybody else.

As she rushed up to the elderly man and greeted him like a long-lost friend, she hoped nobody noticed how astounded he looked.

A few minutes later, she was driving out of the airport behind the wheel of a compact, powder-blue Fiat. As she left the green-swathed terminal building behind, Olivia felt as if she had truly embarked on her adventure. Italy had been on the top of her list of destinations for years, but she'd never thought she'd have the chance to travel here. Since she started work at JCreative, the longest vacation she'd taken had been three and a half days. In any case, Italy hadn't been on Matt's bucket list.

She'd come to terms with the fact that her obsession with Tuscany would never be more than a long-distance relationship, but now, here she was.

To her delight, the countryside was just as she'd imagined. Fields of all shapes and sizes, combed with neat rows of vines, were slotted like puzzle pieces in between olive groves and forests. She glimpsed farmhouses built from honeyed stone, surrounded by clusters of trees. Looking beyond them, she gazed expectantly at the horizon, hoping she might see the coastline of the Tyrrhenian Sea along the way.

Her GPS was working perfectly, navigating her through this picturesque landscape.

Almost perfectly, Olivia amended, as she turned right into the narrow road which was supposed to take her straight through the hillside town of Collina. Instead, the road zigzagged high into the hills.

Where was she now? She peered down at the map and then looked up, realizing with a start that she was being tailgated by a sleek, orange and black sports car.

It was a Bugatti Veyron, she saw in amazement, as the driver overtook her with a throaty growl of his engine, speeding around the next bend and out of sight. She'd never seen one before, but knew they cost millions of dollars and that to a car nut, their performance was worth every cent. She guessed she shouldn't be surprised to see one out on the road in a country where passion for fast, stylish cars was such an integral part of the culture.

She bent to her map again, but her head snapped up hurriedly as she realized there was another car behind her.

This was a police car, lights flashing, clearly in pursuit. It, too, overtook her and went screaming into the hills.

"Hope you catch him," Olivia shouted supportively, even though she didn't think the policeman stood a chance. That Bugatti had shown some serious acceleration.

The GPS had directed her wrong, but her route had taken her up to the most extraordinary hillside village. It must have been a medieval outpost, with high, square towers and narrow buildings with tiny windows, packed together on the hillside. The town itself was a higgledy-piggledy maze of streets. There wasn't room to turn around, and Olivia wondered if she'd ever find her way out again.

She narrowed her eyes in concentration as she squeezed the car around a corner that felt far too tight even for the compact Fiat. In between two high stone walls, there was no wiggle room at all. Olivia held her breath, praying her bumper would survive the experience. She let out a long, relieved sigh when she and her car made it through the space undamaged and she saw the main road ahead.

Her GPS rerouted, directing her down the hill.

Olivia slowed down, staring in fascination as she spotted the Bugatti parked by the roadside, with the police car behind it. The narrow gap and cobbled streets had allowed the law to catch up. What would the driver's penalty be? she wondered. As she passed, she let out a delighted laugh.

The driver and police officer were standing in front of the Bugatti, engaged in an animated and enthusiastic conversation. The police officer had taken his phone out and was snapping photos of the supercar. That looked to have been the only reason for his pursuit.

Only in Italy, Olivia thought, thrilled to have seen this interaction play out.

Rejoining the road, she saw the signpost for Collina ahead. Now to keep a lookout for the villa.

She caught her breath as the imposing entrance came into view, flanked by tall stone gateposts. The wrought iron gate stood open, and she headed up the paved drive to the elegant stone house. Its pillared front porch and high, arched windows were exactly as it had looked in the Instagram picture, but the narrow camera angle hadn't done justice to the breathtaking panorama of gently rolling hills and wooded valleys, the clearness of the azure sky, and the fragrant scent of the warm air.

She parked under a wooden carport, the poles entwined by vines.

Olivia climbed out of the cramped front seat, stretched her arms above her head, and breathed in deeply. Turning slowly, she took in the magnificence of the scenery that surrounded her.

She'd expected it to be beautiful but she hadn't guessed she would feel such a sense of peace on arrival. Somehow, the landscape was familiar and comforting to her, even though she'd never set foot in Italy before.

As she lifted her bag out of the trunk, Olivia decided it was because of her lifelong obsession with the area. No wonder the place already seemed like home.

Suddenly, a two-week vacation felt too short.

She walked up to the wooden front door, flanked by large clay pots filled with vivid pink geraniums.

"Hello?" she called, tapping on the door. "Charlotte, are you here?"

She tried the door, but it was locked.

Olivia frowned, wondering if she had the right villa. Perhaps she hadn't gone far enough up the hill.

Then a fluttering piece of paper in the flowerpot caught her eye.

Olivia picked it up and unfolded it.

"Overslept!" the note read. "Gone to get us lunch! Key is in this pot!"

Looking more closely, Olivia saw the key, half-hidden under a leaf.

Opening the door, she stepped into the pleasantly cool interior. The smooth, tiled floor made her want to kick off her shoes immediately and tread over it barefoot.

Indoor plants positioned near the bay windows in the entrance hall added a splash of greenery. The artwork on the walls must be by a local artist, she thought, because the vivid, rustic paintings captured the patchwork beauty of the fields and trees she'd seen outside. Her eyes were drawn to the high, wooden ceiling, where an ornate chandelier glinted.

Heading down the corridor, Olivia opened the first door on the right, and found herself in the empty bedroom that Charlotte had said was hers. She set her suitcase down at the foot of the large four-poster bed and looked out of the high-arched window.

Her gaze traveled over the fenced vegetable garden to the grassy lawn dotted with fruit trees. Were those pear trees? Pomegranate trees? She couldn't wait to walk out into the sunshine to check.

Wrenching herself away from the window, Olivia headed into the en suite bathroom. The claw-footed bath tempted her to have a long soak, but knowing Charlotte would be back soon, she settled for a quick shower and changed into fresh clothes. She sat for a moment, staring at the faraway horizon. Having this endless view made her appreciate how deep in the countryside they were.

She took out her phone and took a photo for her Instagram.

"#Romanticdestination #impulseholiday #wineterritory #farawayfrom-home," she commented.

She hoped Matt would see. She was sure that after the humiliation of their restaurant break-up, he would be stalking her social media. He'd be visualizing her home alone, mourning his loss and regretting her untidy habits. When he saw the photo of Tuscany, she imagined how his lips would press together and he'd get that strangely thoughtful look in his eyes.

Thinking of Matt made her remember her final day at work and the audacity of what she'd done.

Abruptly, reality rushed in.

Turning away from the view, Olivia drew in a sharp breath.

What had she been thinking?

She'd quit her job without even giving notice. She'd booked an impulse holiday with no thought to her future. Senior positions in the advertising world were scarce—it was a competitive industry, and that fear had always been in the back of her mind every time she'd worked the long hours and put in the overtime and sacrificed her holidays and social life.

Burying her face in her hands, Olivia realized she had thrown it all away. Now she was in another country, on the other side of the world, with no opportunity to do damage control or even ask for her job back.

Acting as she had done, in a mad, hungover moment, could well have jeopardized her entire future.

The click of the front door interrupted Olivia's agonizing. Charlotte had arrived.

CHAPTER SEVEN

Olivia felt her panic subside as she rushed to the front door, overwhelmed by the joy of being with Charlotte again. This was the first time in nearly three years that she'd seen her oldest and best friend.

"You're here!" Charlotte screamed as Olivia rushed over to hug her. "I can't believe you came all this way to join me."

"It's wonderful to see you!"

Charlotte was a head shorter than Olivia. At ten years old, they'd been exactly the same height and it had been easy to pretend that they were twins instead of best friends. At the age of eleven, Olivia had started her growth spurt, which Charlotte had almost completely missed out on. From then on, being twins hadn't worked, but they'd kept up the pretense of being sisters.

With her round face beaming and her long hair shining with russet streaks, Charlotte radiated good humor. Her presence seemed to fill the villa and her cheerful smile lit up the room. In the glow of her sunny personality, Olivia found herself believing that everything might work out, after all.

"Have you seen the villa?" Charlotte lifted the brown paper bags she'd brought inside. "Let me give you a quick tour, and then we can have lunch."

Olivia had only gotten as far as the bedroom before having her panic attack. Eager to explore, she took one of the bags and followed Charlotte down the tiled, airy corridor.

With its terracotta floor tiles and warm, cream-colored walls, the villa felt welcoming and homely. Matt's décor staples had been geometric black and white. Over the past few years, everything in her apartment had gradually become one of the two. White curtains, black rug. Black bedcovers, white pillowcases. Black leather couches, white coffee table. Black, white, white, black ... Olivia had felt as if she were living in a chessboard.

Now, she was captivated by the detail and warmth that surrounded her. Clay pots and terracotta vases stood in arched alcoves along the passageway. Tapestries hung on the walls—depictions of landscapes, food, and wine, framed by wrought iron scrolls.

The two bedrooms were on the right, while on the left, the passageway widened into an open-plan living and dining area. It was sumptuously furnished, with plush, beige leather couches. The coffee table and the dining table were made of richly textured wood.

The centerpiece of the room was the magnificent fireplace at the far end, set in a high, stone-clad wall. Above it, an ornate chandelier sparkled. Lamps with heavy, hand-painted bases and vivid gold and orange shades were dotted around the room on the small tables and shelves. Olivia looked forward to evening, when she would have the fun of turning them on and enjoying the mingled shades of light.

An archway on the left led to the kitchen, and Olivia placed the bag on the counter, admiring the pots of rosemary, thyme, and basil on the wide windowsill that filled the room with their fragrance.

"I bought snacks for lunch, and of course, some wine," Charlotte said.

As she helped arrange the food on the platter, Olivia looked in delight at the brown-paper-wrapped meats, the jars of olives with their exotic Italian labels, the pale, creamy cheese, and the loaf of crusty ciabatta. Once it was all arranged, Olivia couldn't resist taking out her phone and photographing the Instagrammable display.

"Where shall we sit? There's an outside table." Charlotte opened the kitchen door. Beyond, Olivia saw a paved courtyard, framed with beds of herbs and vegetables. A small table and chairs stood at the far end of the courtyard, shaded by the overhanging branch of an olive tree.

"Outside," Olivia decided.

She carried the tray to the small table and sat down on one of the two wrought-iron chairs. The view on this side of the house was equally mesmerizing. The courtyard overlooked the quiet road, beyond which was a golden wheat field. Noticing a grove of trees in the center of the wheat, Olivia remembered from her school days that two thousand years ago, Tuscan farmers had practiced promiscuous agriculture, where their staple crops, usually wheat, olives, and grapes, had been grown together in the same fields.

She'd loved that term. It had been one of the few historical facts that had stuck in her mind from school. Nowadays, it was known as mixed farming, which was nowhere near such an exciting phrase, and the practice wasn't as common as it had been, either.

Beyond the tree-studded wheat field, a distant farmhouse nestled against a backdrop of deep green forest. Looking at it, Olivia felt a pang of envy for the owner. Did they know how lucky they were, living in this charming place?

She suspected this was the first of many similar pangs she would endure during these two weeks. She felt jealous of everyone in this area. All of them!

Charlotte poured the wine and they toasted each other.

"To friendship," Olivia said.

She breathed in the grassy bouquet of the ice-cold Sauvignon Blanc, smiling as she took a sip.

"To impulse holidays," Charlotte said, and they drank again.

"To new beginnings," Olivia added, for a third toast.

"To losing weight," Charlotte concluded.

Olivia raised her eyebrows, staring at the spread of food.

"I've lost a hundred and eighty pounds in the last two weeks," Charlotte explained. "That's approximately what Patrick weighed."

"What happened?" Olivia asked. "You were about to get married."

"I called it off," Charlotte said. She selected a piece of ciabatta bread and slathered it with sundried tomato dip.

"Why was that?" Olivia said, as she built a sandwich with ham, cheese, and olive tapenade. She was curious about what could have gone wrong between Charlotte and her fiancé, whom she'd never met, but who had seemed from his constant presence on Charlotte's Instagram to be good-looking and charming.

Charlotte made a face.

"It was complicated."

She started speaking, stopped, sighed, and had a sip of wine.

"Too complicated for now," she concluded, gesturing impatiently with a piece of Parma ham. "I don't want to spoil our lovely lunch by discussing such a horrible subject."

Olivia nodded sympathetically.

"At any rate, it brought you here," she consoled her friend.

"Exactly," Charlotte agreed. "And it brought you here, too. You were so busy it didn't cross my mind to invite you. Will you have to do any work on your vacation?"

"No," Olivia said. All her fears came rushing back as she added, "I quit."

Charlotte nearly choked on her wine.

"You quit your job? You mean you just walked out?"

"I hated it." Feeling a pang of guilt, Olivia tried to justify her actions. "I was marketing cheap swill wine that goes against everything I believe in."

"Could you not have moved to another account?" Charlotte asked in tones of hushed awe that made Olivia feel even worse. "You told me your mother always said that if you gave up advertising, you wouldn't be qualified to do anything except stocking shelves."

"I need a new career direction. Not shelf stocking," Olivia said firmly. "Vacationing in wine country will give me time to think about it. One of my dreams is to produce my own artisanal wine label."

"I love cats, so one of my dreams is to be a lion tamer." Charlotte laughed merrily, but then saw Olivia's face and her smile vanished. "I thought you were making a joke. You mean it about the wine label?"

"Yes, I do. It's a dream of mine," Olivia insisted. Now that she was here, it seemed even more appealing than it had back in Chicago.

"Wow. Well, for now, do you want to see the garden? The grounds are beautiful."

Eager to explore their surroundings, Olivia stood up, and they headed out into the grounds.

While browsing the villa's website, she'd read that the five acres had originally been used for free range chicken farming. An old wooden chicken coop, placed artfully in the garden, served as a reminder of that fact.

Passing an orchard, they headed up a steep incline and into a grassy field dotted with shrubs and bordered by trees. Olivia wondered if this was where the free range chickens had roamed.

The pathway hugged the border of the overgrown field, and Olivia realized she recognized the trees, thanks to their distinctive thick, fissured bark. They were cork oak. How appropriate to find them here, in wine growing country.

She admired them for a few minutes, running her hands over the bark, before returning to the courtyard, fragrant with herbs.

Olivia walked into the coolness of the kitchen feeling conflicted. One half of her was breathless with wonder at having traveled to this paradise. The other half was quaking with terror that her reckless actions might have jeopardized her entire future.

A friendly pat on her shoulder distracted her from her thoughts.

"You wouldn't be panicking about your job, would you?" Charlotte asked.

"Just a little," Olivia admitted.

Charlotte folded her arms sternly.

"Not allowed on holiday, I'm afraid. Why don't we take a drive around town? There's a local bar that I've been curious about. I've seen lots of gorgeous men going in there. Are you up for it?"

Olivia remembered the dream she'd had before the plane touched down. OK, so that had ended in an embarrassing experience, but that was all the more reason to try again. Somewhere, love was waiting for her, and it wouldn't wait forever.

"Let me put on some lipstick, and I'll be ready to go!" she agreed.

CHAPTER EIGHT

As they headed into the small town of Collina, Olivia was glad that Charlotte was at the wheel. She was so captivated by the scenery that she would probably have driven them straight into one of the stone walls that lined the narrow street.

There was a ruined castle outside the town entrance—a real castle with crumbling walls and battlements on its tower. It looked dark and imposing, silhouetted against the low, late afternoon sun. Perhaps, long ago, this tower had guarded the village from invaders.

Imagine living next door to a real, live, ruined castle. She suffered her second pang of envy of the day, as she eyeballed the nearby two-story apartments with their faded cream facades, wooden shutters, and colorful flower boxes under the windows.

As she watched, a young woman holding a shopping basket hurried down the staircase, calling a cheery, *"Buon giorno,"* to her neighbor. Her long dark hair was tied back in a ponytail and she was dressed with the natural sense of style that Olivia had realized every Italian seemed to possess. Never in a million years could Olivia pair that deep burgundy top with sky blue, calf-length jeans and bright white sandals, and look as if she'd stepped straight out of the pages of *Vogue.*

On her, the clothes would seem mismatched, as if she'd chosen them while groping in the dark. People would stare at the shoes and then up at her as if to say, Really? Those?

In the town itself, a wrought-iron railing separated the narrow pedestrian walkway from the almost-as-narrow road. Leaning out of the car window, Olivia breathed in the rich aroma of coffee from the corner shop. Even though it was late afternoon, a few locals were at the counter, drinking espressos and reading their phones.

Everybody except her and Charlotte looked as if they lived and belonged here. What a privilege to see the locals going about their everyday life in this out-of-the-way spot.

Spying a small clothing boutique, Olivia wondered if she should dare to visit it, and see if she could acquire some Italian style with the store assistant's help. She was pleased to see a wine shop doing a busy trade. Beyond it was a shoe shop, a vegetable kiosk with a bright, colorful display of tomatoes and mandarins outside, a hairdresser, and a tiny hardware outlet and grocery store.

Two bakeries across the road from each other were closing their shutters for the day.

"Do you think they're rivals?" Charlotte asked, stopping to allow an elderly man to cross the road.

"I'm sure they are," Olivia said, glancing back and forth between the two signs. "They practically have to be. The feud probably goes back centuries."

"And one day when the son of Mazetti's owner falls in love with the daughter of Forno Collina's owner, they will have to elope to Pisa and their families will disown them forever," Charlotte elaborated on the story.

At that moment a man in a white apron walked out of Mazetti's. He glared at the shop opposite and then marched across the road. Taking his phone out of his pocket, he began photographing the "On Special" signs displayed in the other shop's window.

Olivia and Charlotte collapsed with laughter.

"They really are rivals!" Olivia snorted. "Tomorrow morning he'll be undercutting those prices, or copying the package deals. He's noticed us—let's drive on before we get caught up in this drama."

At the end of what passed for the town's main street was a tiny church with an ornate spire. The gray-haired pastor stood outside, sweeping the stone stairs. He nodded a greeting as they passed, and Olivia smiled back, charmed. Her first day in Italy, and she was already being accepted by the locals.

Turning around at the end of the town, Charlotte drove to the small, bustling bar which was situated up a steeply sloping cul-de-sac. The street was crammed with cars and there were no parking spaces to be seen. Olivia was starting to realize why everyone drove such small cars. Space, everywhere, was at a premium. When she'd first climbed into the Fiat she'd thought it was tiny after the large sedans and SUVs she'd been used to back home. Now, she saw that it was sensibly sized for the area, quite spacious in fact.

Although, as Charlotte swore, trying to turn her rented Fiat around in the nonexistent space, Olivia started wishing that the car was even smaller.

After completing a roughly thirty-six-point turn, Charlotte made it without any damage to the bumpers or hubcaps.

They drove all the way back down the hill and parked in another, quieter street, before returning on foot.

The thumping beat of music drew them up the hill again, and Olivia marveled at how even Italian rock sounded melodious thanks to the beauty of the language. She reminded herself that learning some phrases would be a priority. Perhaps they could make a start tonight, right here in this bar.

Olivia breathed in the combined aroma of beer, wine, cigarette smoke, and—she was sure—testosterone. A soccer game was playing on a screen above the bar. To her delight, she couldn't pick up a word of English in the babble of conversation. This was most definitely a bar for locals.

There was a pause as the regulars took in the two new arrivals. Olivia noticed some appreciative glances coming their way.

They hadn't even reached the bar counter before they were greeted by two men, perched on bar stools at a tiny round table.

"*Ciao!*" the closest man called.

Olivia's heart skipped as she looked around. The roguish-looking man was around thirty years old, with dark hair and heavy brows and a wicked smile. His friend looked a few years older, shaven-headed and deeply tanned.

"Er—*ciao*," she replied. She glanced at Charlotte, who gave her a conspiratorial smile.

Then the man spoke in rapid Italian.

Olivia spread her hands. "*Non comprehendo?*" she tried.

"Ah. *Americano.*"

More Italian was spoken and after a shouted conversation with the surrounding tables, two more stools were lifted over the crowd.

"Giuseppe," the man said, pointing to himself. "Alfredo," he introduced his friend.

"Olivia. I'm sorry I don't speak Italian. I've only just arrived here," Olivia apologized, perching on the proffered seat as Charlotte introduced herself.

"Welcome, Olivia." Giuseppe grinned. "Er—Carlotta?"

Charlotte's name caused more difficulties with the locals than hers, Olivia realized.

"Wine? Red, white?"

"Red, please."

In the crowded space, she was squashed against Giuseppe's muscular arm. Charlotte and Alfredo seemed to be getting on famously. As for herself, with Matt no longer in her life, she was more than ready for some light flirtation. Who knew where it might lead?

"You are very beautiful," Giuseppe complimented her, and Olivia found herself blushing. Did he really think so? Could this be the start of a whirlwind holiday romance?

"Where are you staying?" he asked.

"I'm staying in a nearby villa. I'm on a two-week vacation," Olivia said.

The wine was delicious, bursting with ripe fruitiness and a hint of spice. Drinking it made her think of the mural on the villa's kitchen wall, a collage of vivid, purple-red grapes.

"Do you live here?" Olivia asked, eager to learn his role within this idyllic setting.

Giuseppe shook his head. "No, not here."

"You work here, then?" Perhaps he lived in another village, Olivia thought.

Giuseppe gave her another flashing smile. "Also, no."

"Ah," Olivia said, momentarily at a loss. "What do you do?"

Since he didn't live or work in the town, she guessed he might be an artisanal winemaker, tirelessly laboring on his own small vineyard in the warm Mediterranean rays. That fit in perfectly with her life goal. Imagine if the holiday romance turned into something more. One day, they might even work his land together, as a couple. She imagined sunny days on the farm with him, pressing the grapes in an airy shed, creating limited-edition wines of unique quality and character.

"I am a cleaner," Giuseppe explained.

"A cleaner?" Olivia felt taken aback. A cleaner didn't fit so well into the rural fantasy she'd visualized. In fact, it was the wrong puzzle piece entirely. Her fantasy had stalled.

"Do you work at a wine farm?" she asked, bravely trying to restart it.

"No. I clean toilets on a cruise ship," Guiseppe said. "The ship is docked in Livorno tonight, so I am visiting with my cousin." He indicated Alfredo, deep in conversation with Charlotte.

"I see." Olivia's smile felt suddenly forced. Toilets?

"Perhaps we can go back to your place now. For coffee?" Giuseppe grinned again, eagerly. "We must hurry, because I have to be back on board by five a.m."

Her dreams of romance had shattered.

Never mind a holiday fling, Giuseppe was only in town for a night. That wasn't what she'd visualized when she'd caught his eye. It wasn't what she wanted at all!

At that moment, she heard Charlotte's outraged cry.

"No! Absolutely not! You know what, I'm outta here. Olivia, come on!"

Surprised, but relieved, Olivia scrambled off her chair, waving a hasty good-bye to Giuseppe as Charlotte grabbed her arm and marched her out of the bar.

What had happened to cause Charlotte to storm off so suddenly?

Questions would have to wait. It was all Olivia could do to keep up with her angry friend as she hustled down the hill.

CHAPTER NINE

"What went wrong?" Olivia asked Charlotte breathlessly, as they rounded a corner.

"That Alfredo! Do you know what he said?" Charlotte sounded irate. "He said that seeing I was a rich Americano, I should pay for the first round of drinks!"

"What?" Olivia asked incredulously. "But he invited you to sit down. That doesn't mean you buy the round. What nerve."

"I am furious. Furious!" Charlotte stomped along the cobbled walkway. "What gives him the right to assume that I'd be paying? I ask you!"

As they headed back to the car at record-breaking speed, Olivia wondered whether Charlotte's anger was only due to Alfredo's presumptuousness.

She suspected there might be another reason for her response, and resolved to ask her friend about it as soon as she had calmed down enough, because she'd never seen her overreact that way before.

For some reason, Alfredo's actions had triggered Charlotte.

As they arrived back at the villa, Olivia's phone started to ring.

"Who's calling so late?" she wondered aloud to Charlotte, as it was almost nine p.m.

Then she realized two details.

Firstly, she wasn't late in the States, where they were about seven hours behind.

Secondly, it was her mother on the line.

"Oh, damn," Olivia said, her heart sinking.

She hadn't told her mother that she'd broken up with Matt, or quit her job, or hopped on a plane for an impulse holiday in a foreign country.

This was going to be a tough phone call. Questioning Charlotte would have to wait.

"Hello, Mom," Olivia said, trying to sound cheerful as she answered the call.

She went straight to the fridge, hoping another glass of wine would help her manage this conversation.

It would be better not to say too much, Olivia decided. Her mother was too highly strung to be able to cope with a triple bombshell. She should break the news gently, over a period of days, one shock at a time.

Olivia wished that she had a better relationship with her mother, but they'd never been close. Her mother had led a sheltered life, marrying young, and had tried to live vicariously through Olivia.

That, unfortunately, meant trying to interfere in a lot of her life choices.

"Olivia!" Her mother's voice was quivering with tension. "What's happening? Have you broken up with Matt?"

"Um, why do you ask that?"

Her plans lay in ruins. Her mother already knew about bombshell number one. Olivia put the phone on speaker and poured wine into two glasses.

"Edna saw he'd changed his status to Single. She called me just now."

Olivia felt irate. How dare Matt change his status to Single, when the truth was he should have made it Cheating?

"It was an amicable break-up. A mutual decision," she lied.

Apart from having a stand-up fight in the middle of a fancy restaurant. Otherwise, totally amicable.

"Olivia!" her mother gasped. "You broke up with Matt? Do you have any idea what you've done?"

"It was more his idea, actually," Olivia tried, but Mrs. Glass was unstoppable.

"I always felt you didn't value your relationship with him. I don't think you appreciated what a dynamic young man he was. And wealthy, too, Olivia, that counts for a lot. Men like Matt don't grow on trees. You were foolhardy to throw that chance away. You should have married him."

"Mom!" Olivia said, outraged.

Sitting opposite, Charlotte rolled her eyes in sympathy.

Olivia picked up her wine glass and took a large swallow of the delicious white.

"What's that sound?" Mrs. Glass asked. "Olivia, are you drinking? It sounds like you're busy drinking wine."

"Yes, I'm having a glass," Olivia confessed, feeling ashamed. Her mother seemed to have an uncanny knack for making her feel that way.

"It's not even two p.m. on a working day? Is everything all right? Do you need to go to counseling? Olivia, you must be careful or you could lose your job. Day drinking is very dangerous."

"I quit my job," Olivia said. This wasn't how she had intended the conversation to go, but there seemed no way back now.

Mrs. Glass drew a sharp breath.

"You quit your job? When? Why?"

"On Friday. I just walked out. I couldn't do it anymore. It was destroying me," Olivia tried to explain.

"It was a good, well-paying job." Mrs. Glass sounded on the point of tears. "Jobs like that are scarce. Do you have any idea what you've done?"

With a guilty twinge, Olivia thought that perhaps she hadn't.

"It may not be easy to get another. You just walked out? You didn't even give thirty days' notice?"

"I'd had enough," Olivia repeated firmly.

"You may not have any prospects now in such a saturated job market. The advertising world is too competitive. There'll be someone else waiting to take your place."

Olivia pressed her fingers into her temples.

"I'll be fine," she muttered.

If she ever developed a day drinking problem, she was beginning to realize what the trigger might be.

She took another swallow of wine, replacing the glass with the tiniest of clinks, uneasily aware that her mother had probably intuited what she was doing, even if she hadn't heard.

"Olivia, do you want to come and stay with us for a while? I don't believe you're thinking clearly."

"I'm fine. Really, I am."

"Miranda's daughter has just opened a beauty spa in Milwaukee. I know you don't have any beauty qualifications, but there are two receptionist positions."

"Mom, I—"

"I think they were looking for women under twenty-five—you know, fresh-faced, but they might make an exception for you if I explain how desperate you are. And you're young for your age. You don't look a day over thirty-three. You have your grandmother's skin. Of course, she also battled with her hair falling out. Alopecia. By seventy she was practically bald. You haven't experienced that yet, have you, angel?"

Olivia plucked at her blond locks nervously. Was her hair thinning?

"I can't say I have."

"It's probably still coming," her mother said. "But anyway, there are options, and I do believe you need to start investigating them."

"I'll buy an anti-hair-loss shampoo," Olivia promised.

"No, no, sweetheart. I meant job options. That's what I'm worried about."

"Thank you, Mom." Olivia decided the best way to end this conversation was to agree with her mother.

"I'll speak to Miranda tomorrow. Would you be able to attend an interview this week, if there's still a position available?"

Across the table, Charlotte buried her head in her hands.

"Not this week," Olivia said. She took a deep breath. "I'm in Italy."

There was a short, shocked pause.

"There's something wrong with this line. I thought I heard you say you were in Italy," her mother said faintly.

"I am. I'm sharing a villa in Tuscany for two weeks. With Charlotte. Remember Charlotte?" Olivia threw her friend's name into the conversation, hoping it would distract her mother from the impact of bombshell number three.

There was a stunned silence.

"Olivia, have you lost your mind? This is not the time to be jetting off on vacation. It's financially irresponsible. You should be looking for a new position immediately, not wasting money on overseas travel." She raised her voice. "Andrew, can you believe what Olivia's done? She's gone off to Italy for two weeks." In a normal tone, she continued. "My angel, I don't think this is wise."

Olivia didn't have the strength to continue arguing. What was it about her mother? When she got that dramatic note into her voice, there was nobody who could fight against it. It was better simply to agree.

"I will explore other options, I promise, Mom. I'll send out my CV tomorrow. And I have a big bonus which is being paid today."

"Olivia." The dramatic tone was still audible. There was no budging it now. "I want you to promise me that you will have at least one job interview lined up by the time you get home."

"I promise," Olivia said in a small voice.

She disconnected the call, picked up her wineglass, and downed the remainder in one gulp.

She forced herself to remember that she had been independent for thirteen years, and that this was roughly the eighty-fifth time that her mother had predicted an incipient catastrophe in Olivia's life.

"I guess that was expected," she told Charlotte.

"Your mother does not cope well with surprises," Charlotte agreed.

"My father's more adaptable."

"I wouldn't know about that," Charlotte said. "I can't recall ever hearing him speak."

Olivia sighed.

Charlotte wagged her finger at her friend.

"Don't you start second-guessing your decision. Bless your mom's heart and I know she has the best intentions, but I can see she has planted a seed of doubt in your mind."

"No, truly, she hasn't," Olivia protested.

But she knew, deep down, that her mother had.

CHAPTER TEN

Olivia woke with sun streaming in through her window. Outside was a view of the faraway hills, combed by green rows of vines. On the wide windowsill was a flowering plant, its yellow blossoms bright in the morning rays.

She knew she should feel happy, but all she could think of was her mother's warning.

It was as if those darkly dramatic intonations had penetrated her subconscious, and now she imagined money pouring out of her bank account like bathwater after the plug was pulled.

Remembering the dire words about the saturated job market, Olivia wondered what would happen if there was no work available at any of the Chicago agencies.

She got out of bed and rested her hands on the smooth, whitewashed sill of the arched window, staring out at the verdant landscape.

For a moment she was able to forget the doomsday scenario her mother had painted, and lose herself in the incredible view. Here, in this isolated villa with its total privacy, far away from the busy world, she would have some quiet time to think about her future. That was the beauty of solitude.

"Buon giorno!"

A cheerful voice interrupted her thoughts.

The spiky-haired man pushing a wheelbarrow past her window looked about twenty years old, and was wearing faded jeans and a white gym vest.

He was wearing a lot more than she was.

Horrified, Olivia met his gaze and saw his wide, appreciative smile.

She dived to the floor, her face flaming.

"Damn it!" she muttered, as she leopard crawled across the room and grabbed her T-shirt off the chair, pulling it over her head.

So the villa had a gardening service? She should have realized that the grounds received basic care, or else they would have grown completely wild. What a time to find out, though.

Still on her hands and knees, Olivia collected more clothes and crawled into the bathroom. There, with an embarrassed sigh, she got to her feet, grateful for the frosted glass in the bathroom window.

She hoped that she wouldn't have to come face to face with the gardener again. At least, not until she had stopped wanting to hide under the bed every time she thought about it.

Ten years should do it, Olivia decided.

The aroma of freshly brewed coffee drew her out of her room and along the passage to the kitchen.

"Morning," Charlotte said. "Cappuccino or espresso?"

"Cappuccino, please," Olivia said. Remembering how angry Charlotte had been last night, she decided to question her friend. If something was bothering her, Olivia needed to know what it was.

"You were very upset when we left the bar yesterday," she began. "Is there anything you want to share?"

Charlotte sighed.

"It has to do with my ex," she confessed.

Olivia nodded understandingly. Breaking off an engagement when the wedding was just a few weeks away was a drastic decision. Something must have gone very wrong.

"He was a lovely guy—handsome, charming. He seemed like the whole package when I met him," Charlotte said.

Olivia had never met Patrick, but she nodded wisely. Of course, there was going to be a big "but" coming along.

"But," Charlotte said, "there were a few red flags. Like, he didn't work. He thought he was too special to get a job. He lived off his family trust fund, but it wasn't nearly enough. That meant he lived off me."

"Oh, no," Olivia said. "That must have been a very imbalanced relationship."

"I started feeling used," Charlotte said. "We fought about it often. I thought marriage would fix it, and then I realized—oh, hello, Eduardo."

Olivia spun round, slopping her cappuccino into the saucer as the gardener walked in. She felt herself turn bright red.

"Eduardo, this is my friend Olivia, who's staying for a while. Eduardo looks after gardens in the area. He comes here once a week," Charlotte said.

"I think I might have seen you earlier this morning," Olivia admitted, shamefaced.

Eduardo smiled gallantly. "I recall greeting somebody, yes," he said in strongly accented but good English. "However, your room was very dark. I did not see anything clearly."

Olivia remembered the sun streaming in, dazzling her with its brightness.

"You're right, it was very dark," she agreed gratefully.

"Too dark to see much at all," Eduardo added, as if this guaranteed there was no way he had caught even a glimpse of Olivia's uncovered skin.

Charlotte stared at them in confusion before glancing out at the sunny courtyard.

"Come with me," Eduardo invited them. "I must show you something, here, in the villa's grounds."

Olivia exchanged a glance with Charlotte. What could it be?

They followed Eduardo through the courtyard, where he grasped a basket from a wooden shelf. He led them past the fruit trees, their branches heavy with ripening pomegranates and pears, and up a hill.

This was the field they'd walked past yesterday.

Now, as Eduardo guided them in, Olivia saw a faint pathway leading through the wild grasses. Red poppies nodded their heads among the dense grasses, and Olivia spotted white roses and gorse growing near an untamed hedge. She followed Eduardo through the meadow, insects buzzing around her and the long grass tickling her ankles.

Further on, she saw a tiny outbuilding, with stone walls and a tin roof. Near it, almost invisible in the long grass, was a wrought iron bench.

"Look here," Eduardo said.

Shading her eyes against the bright morning sun, Olivia stared in the direction he was pointing. She caught her breath.

Ahead, on the other side of the outbuilding, was a row of tall, healthy grapevines.

"Oh, look at this!"

All her dreams came rushing back as Olivia walked up to the tall, sturdy vines. They hadn't been tended, and looked wild and leafy, but they were filled with fruit. The deep purple grapes had a vivid color and a dusty sheen. She reached out her hand and felt the weight of the bunch. The fruit was warm in the morning sun.

"I wonder what they are," she murmured.

Charlotte made a silly face at her.

"They're grapes, of course. Can't you tell?"

"No, no." Laughing, Olivia hastened to explain. "I meant what type. Like, are they Cabernet or Merlot or—or one of the others?" She was embarrassed to realize she couldn't, at that moment, remember the names of any of the others.

She picked one, knowing this was an experience she'd treasure all her life. She'd done winery tours in the past, each one a memorable treat, but never had she, or any other of the tourists, been allowed near the precious vines that they had viewed from a respectful distance.

The grape's skin was surprisingly tough, and although the flesh was sweet and juicy, Olivia was surprised by the amount of pips. With seedless grapes the norm in the supermarkets, this was something she wasn't used to. She wished she knew more about the role that the skin, and even the pips, played.

"These are ripe," Eduardo told her. "Now is the time when you can pick them, if you like."

He winked at Olivia before walking back down the hill.

An idea occurred to Olivia, so sudden and compelling it was like an epiphany.

"Charlotte, we could make homemade wine! These are clearly wine grapes, and look how many there are. I'm sure we could get at least a bottle, or even two bottles, from the yield on these few vines."

Excitement filled her. What an experience this would be! This could be more than just a holiday adventure. It was the perfect opportunity to take the first step into a world where she'd always wanted to go. She might even find she was naturally talented at it. Although, if winemaking was anything like cooking, she would probably find that she failed numerous times and had to work hard to get it right, Olivia decided more realistically. Still, she'd never know if she didn't try.

"I think it's a great idea," Charlotte said.

They began picking the grapes, filling the basket with the ripe, heavy bunches.

"You do know, though, that the wine will take a few months to be ready?" Charlotte asked.

Olivia stared at her in consternation.

"A few months? But I'm only here for two weeks. Are you sure it takes that long?"

Charlotte nodded. "One time we tried to make pineapple wine, so I remember the process."

"You did? How did it work out?" Olivia asked.

Charlotte shrugged. "It was pretty disgusting, if you must know. We threw it away."

"Perhaps pineapple wasn't the right choice," Olivia ventured. Privately, she thought it sounded disgusting right from the start. Pineapple had no place in wine. In her opinion, it didn't even have a place on pizza.

"If our wine works out, perhaps you could bring a bottle home. We have to taste it together," she told Charlotte.

Olivia brushed a blond lock out of her eyes before moving to the next vine. This one seemed to have an even better yield. She was surprised by how prolifically the grapes grew. She counted nine bunches on this plant alone. Olivia guessed this was why vineyards didn't need a lot of space to produce their wines.

"I just had an even better idea," Charlotte said.

"What's that?"

"You could stay for the whole summer. That will be enough time for the wine to mature. It's not like you have any commitments back home. This is as free as you're ever going to be."

"But I—"

"It would mean a lot if you stayed. I've been lonely here," Charlotte said. "Plus, you can stop me from feeling sorry for Patrick and getting back together. It's happened before."

Olivia considered the invitation from every angle.

Stay in Tuscany the entire summer? It was a crazy idea. Booking for two weeks had felt reckless, as if she were stealing time away from what she should be doing. But what was that?

Staring down at the basket, piled high with bunches of grapes, Olivia assessed her life.

She didn't have a boyfriend, she didn't have a job, she didn't even have a house plant. She had zero commitments back home, and her friend needed her here. Thanks to her bonus, she could pay the bills, and in any case, the job market was always slower over the summer season.

It might be advantageous to wait until the Valley Wines campaign had run its course, and then she could make a fresh start.

Perhaps fate was intervening, Olivia thought. This generous offer, combined with the cushion of money her bonus would provide, might allow her to change the direction of her life completely. She could learn more about wine-making and even offer her unpaid help at one of the local vineyards. It could become a working holiday which might lead to other opportunities. Life didn't offer many chances at a 180-degree turnaround. This was hers, and she should seize it.

Olivia took a deep breath.

"All right," she said, feeling elated and scared and reckless all at once. "I'll do it. I'll commit to staying for the whole summer, but I insist on paying half the villa's rental costs. Now, we need to get these grapes back to the kitchen, and then see how to turn them into wine."

An hour later, Olivia headed down the hill on foot, with a shopping bag in one hand and a long list in the other. She'd opted to walk because although the equipment she needed was bulky, it didn't seem to be heavy. Since the villa was only a mile from town, navigating the narrow, cobbled alleyways in search of parking wasn't worth the risk to the Fiat's side mirrors.

In any case, walking made her feel like a local.

She headed past the ruined castle, enjoying the chance to admire it again. With the evening light behind it, the tower had looked shadowy and foreboding. Now, with the morning sun spilling onto it, the stones were drenched in gold and it looked like a friendlier place. A family castle, rather than a foreboding dungeon.

Her walk took her past the bakeries and she detoured into Mazetti's, lured by the mouthwatering aroma of freshly baked bread. Inside, she chose a golden, crisp-baked ciabatta loaf, and paused at a display of tasty-looking Ricciarelli cookies. The small, oval treats had prettily cracked surfaces and were coated in powdered sugar. They smelled deliciously of almond. Olivia wished she'd had breakfast before embarking on her shopping trip, because this sight was making her hungry.

She glanced at the bakery opposite the road, wondering for an amused moment if exactly the same display of cookies, at the same price, would be on the shelves of Forno Collina, too.

"Try one, please," the baker invited her.

Who could turn down that offer? Not her. She took one and bit into it, enjoying the sweetness of the sugar and the contrast between the crunchy, meringue-like outside and the dense, chewy inside. Almond and orange flavors exploded onto her tongue. These were delicious.

"I'll have twelve, please. Actually, twenty-four," she amended. Better to be realistic—twelve would be gone in a flash.

She walked out of the bakery, resolving not to detour anywhere else, and broke her resolution a moment later when she passed the wine shop.

It was impossible to shop for winemaking supplies without buying some of the finished product, she decided.

This shop was filled with wines she'd never heard of, their labels fascinating and unique. Most of the produce seemed to be from the local area, with the word "Toscana" featuring prominently. Looking at the labels, Olivia realized the most common local grapes were a variety called Sangiovese, which imparted cherry flavors to wine. She wondered if the grapes at the villa were Sangiovese. By the law of averages, she guessed they would be.

Unable to stop herself, Olivia purchased a bottle of local Chianti, made from Sangiovese grapes.

Her shopping basket was already half full, and she hadn't even reached her destination, which was the small hardware store at the far end of the village. This was where Eduardo had explained they could buy winemaking supplies.

In the hardware store, she prowled the narrow aisles, reading her list with eagle eyes as she loaded her basket. She was determined this project was going to be successful.

There seemed to be a lot of amateur winemakers in the area, because there was a whole section of the store dedicated to the equipment. However, the language barrier and her own lack of knowledge proved to be the problem.

It was all very well reading "Wine Hydrometer" scribbled confidently on her list. But what on earth did it look like? And what was the Italian word for it? As Olivia puzzled over the items, the motherly store attendant picked up on her mission and came to her rescue.

Although she had no English, she placed the items that Olivia needed on the counter.

"*Bottiglia?*" she asked, pointing to the glass bottles stacked high up on the shelf.

That was the only item Olivia knew she didn't need.

Using expressive arm gestures and pantomiming, she was able to convey to the attendant that no, she and her friend were enthusiastic wine drinkers who would have more than enough empty bottles by the time the wine was made; in fact, probably too many.

The woman laughed uproariously, nodding approval as she rang the items up.

Olivia handed over her bank card. She'd expected the transaction to go without a hitch, but to her concern, the woman shook her head.

"*Carta rifiutata,*" she said, handing it back, and her regretful expression told Olivia exactly what the phrase meant.

She felt her heart accelerate. What had gone wrong? Although she was always broke by mid-month, and had to rely on her trusty credit card, she'd thought this month would be different, thanks to the back pay and massive bonus that should be in her account today.

She'd hoped that dipping into her credit card would be a thing of the past.

If her salary and bonus had not been paid, that meant something had gone badly wrong. Salaries were always paid on time at JCreative. Always.

She'd have to dip into her credit card again and try to figure out the problem when she was back at the villa.

She handed the credit card over with a smiling apology, but she had to force the smile.

Inside, she felt frantic with worry. She'd been relying on that money. She needed it. She'd already made commitments, assuming it would be paid.

There were two reasons she could think of for the non-appearance of her money.

Firstly, there had been some unforeseen problem with the payment which could be sorted out.

Secondly, and more seriously, James was withholding it on purpose. That possibility filled her with dread, and she hoped that it was wrong.

James was a nasty boss some of the time, but he was a terrible adversary all of the time. When he had his guns out for somebody, Olivia had always felt glad she was sitting on his side of the boardroom table.

Now, she feared, her own actions might have put her on the opposite side.

She hurried home, anxious to find out if her salary would be paid at all, and whether she had ended up in James's crosshairs.

CHAPTER ELEVEN

Back at the villa, Olivia checked the time. It was still too early in the States to call the agency. Even though rumor had it that James only slept three hours a night, he usually arrived at work at six a.m.

Quickly, she composed a polite email asking about her money and sent it to him, copying the accounting manager.

Then Olivia did her best to put her fear aside. She didn't want any negative thoughts contaminating her first ever batch of wine. For all she knew, this could be a stunning success. It could springboard her into a brand new life and career.

The first step was to wash and crush the grapes. She turned on the kitchen tap and carefully washed each bunch of grapes. As she did so, she removed the grapes from their bunches, and the stems from the grapes, just like the Internet had told her to.

She was sure she could trust the Internet for this important project. The recipe had numerous five-star reviews. Although, when Olivia had started reading the reviews, they'd all said things like: "Excellent recipe! I tweaked it slightly by adding a bottle of brandy to the finished product," and "This worked out really well! We made a few changes and produced chocolate wine by mixing drinking chocolate into the second fermentation."

Olivia decided she was going to stick to the basic recipe as strictly as she could. No brandy, no chocolate, no anything except the exquisite, probably Sangiovese, Tuscan grapes.

While the grapes drained, Olivia used the disinfectant she'd bought to thoroughly clean all the equipment.

Then she and Charlotte pulled on latex gloves, and with the help of a sieve, got to work crushing the grapes by hand, pouring the juice into the container where the primary fermentation would take place.

"It's hard labor doing this," Charlotte remarked as they each moved to their second bunch. "Messy, too. I feel like a real daughter of the soil. Oops," she said, as a grape squirted sideways, the juice staining her shirt.

Olivia checked her own shirt. Probably, a white top hadn't been the best choice. It was already covered in pale pink spatters. While she was looking down, a grape squirted her in the eye.

"Ouch," she said, blinking furiously. "I think I have poor crushing technique. Further safety equipment is needed."

Olivia ran to the bedroom and came back with her sunglasses. She decided they would offer workspace eye protection, and also prevent her from noticing the buildup of stains on the now-pink front of her top.

Not only was the work tricky, but also time consuming. While she was enjoying the novelty, she had to admit it was not proceeding at a productive pace. In fact, she was beginning to wonder if the large pile of grapes that they had optimistically picked would ever be crushed.

"What are we going to call our wine? It has to have a name, right?" Charlotte asked.

"First things first," Olivia laughed. "We need the batch to work out."

"Seeing you're the English major, you should choose. Why not give the wine a literary name?" Charlotte mused.

"Grape Expectations?" Olivia suggested.

"I was not thinking along those lines."

Olivia tried again. "Wined in the Willows?"

They started to laugh.

"Maybe we shouldn't name it yet," Charlotte said. "There seems to be a lack of focus from certain members of the naming committee."

"And certain members of the winemaking committee are skipping important steps, like the manufacturing process," Olivia cautioned. "It might not be as easy as we think. Let's not count our chickens before they've hatched, or our wine before it's fermented."

Finally, the grapes were all crushed. The fermenter was half-full of glowing, ruby liquid, the kitchen table was covered in sticky stains, and the discarded grape skins were piled up in a large bucket.

Looking at the results of their efforts, Olivia felt thrilled.

Using mental arithmetic, she calculated the amount of yeast that was needed for the size of this batch, and added it.

As Olivia fastened the lid onto the container, her phone rang.

Twisting the lid hurriedly into place, she rushed to answer.

It was James on the line.

Quickly, she grabbed the call, crossing her fingers in the hope of a successful outcome.

"Hi, James. Did you see my email?"

"Your email? Yes, I did read it, Olivia," he said.

Olivia had hoped that he'd be calling to tell her he'd authorized the wire, but his tone of voice was worrying her. He sounded guarded and yet smug. She'd heard that note in his voice in the past, usually as he announced that they'd won a major victory over an opposition agency.

"I'm shocked by what you told me," he added.

"I was surprised, too," she said, relieved that she'd been worrying for no reason, and that James was on her side. "I didn't mean to get anyone in trouble, but I thought I should notify you about the delay."

To her shame, she realized she had adopted the same brisk, businesslike tone that she'd used to impress him while she was working there. She was hopeless, just hopeless. Olivia felt amazed all over again that she'd managed to find the courage to leave.

"That's not why I was shocked," James continued, and now Olivia felt a shiver of doubt, because his words sounded like a whiplash.

"I—" she began, but he kept talking right over her.

"What effrontery! I cannot believe the bare-faced audacity of your mail. Did you think that you could walk out on this company, and then demand money after breaking the terms of your contract?"

"The terms?" Olivia asked faintly.

"Thirty calendar days' notice is mandatory for both parties."

Her eyes widened. That wasn't how things worked. James had fired many people for arbitrary reasons, and never once had any of them been given thirty days' notice. Even the people who handed in a written resignation letter were ordered off the premises immediately.

"The money was due to me," she pleaded. "I'd already earned it. It was back pay and bonus money, and I'd had a letter saying it was going to be paid."

"I met with my lawyer this morning. He told me there are valid grounds for canceling the payment, due to your dereliction of duty," James shot back. "You walked out at a crucial moment. It could have cost the company millions. As it happens, Kansas Foods signed the deal, but it could have jeopardized everything."

"But they signed. So what's the problem? You didn't need me," she tried.

"I'm not going to argue. You're not getting that money. And I hope you think twice before letting anyone else down the same way." His voice sharpened. "Not that you'll have the chance. I've already notified a few of my closest colleagues, by which I mean the top twenty agencies in Chicago, about your appalling and unethical behavior."

"James, you—" Olivia felt suddenly sick.

"So, unless you manage to find a job stocking shelves, I sure hope your rich boyfriend will be prepared to pay your expenses from here on." Now a note of bitter satisfaction crept into his voice. "Although from what I see on social media, he came to his senses and dumped you, too. Goodbye, Olivia."

He disconnected, leaving Olivia clutching her phone in horror.

This was a disaster of epic proportions. James had canceled the money due to her. That massive bonus that she'd worked so hard for had vanished into thin air. Nothing would be paid.

She would have to fly back and mount a legal challenge against the company. Olivia doubted it would be successful. James had a top legal team on retainer. Olivia didn't even have a lawyer. She'd never used one, never sued anyone.

She was bitterly aware that all she'd end up doing was getting herself deeper into debt, but she had no choice. Desperate times called for desperate measures. At any rate, she couldn't stay in Italy any longer. There was no way she could contribute half the villa's costs.

"Aaargh," she said, blinking tears out of her eyes.

"What's up?"

Freshly showered and changed, Charlotte hurried back into the kitchen.

"There's been a catastrophe," Olivia said. "I'm going to have to go home."

"Oh, no. What is it?" Wide-eyed with concern, Charlotte sat down next to her.

"James is refusing to pay the money I'm owed. This means I'm broke. I'm going to have to go back and fight for it."

Olivia stared at the fermenter that she'd filled with such excitement. Now she'd have to say goodbye to her first ever batch of wine, and to the villa, and to Tuscany.

She should have known this would happen. Her silly idea about embarking on a new career in wine had been just that—a stupid, impossible, and unrealistic dream. She'd hoped to do a 180-degree turnaround and instead she'd gone 360 degrees, and ended up facing the same way she'd started, only with fewer prospects.

What a disaster.

"Oh, Olivia, that's too terrible," Charlotte soothed her. "Please don't rush home. Wait until you're feeling less panicked and can think about this with a clear head."

Olivia nodded reluctantly. Charlotte's advice was sensible. Acting in panic would be a mistake.

"Let's go out and do some wine tasting," her friend urged. "You need to cheer up and put some distance between yourself and your problems. And whatever happens, visiting these estates is going to be a bucket-list adventure."

As they drove out of the villa, Olivia paged through the wine farm brochures stashed in the Fiat's cubbyhole. There were two famous estates in the area. One was close by, and the other on the far side of the village.

The names alone sounded enchanting. Casa D'Orio and La Leggenda. Staring at the glossy photographs, she forced her anxiety to subside. This was a once-in-a-lifetime experience, and she wasn't going to let James's toxic actions ruin it.

She decided she would make the call tomorrow about what to do, and when to leave. Perhaps today's adventures would bring a sign, something to help her decide.

Which vineyard to choose first?

She had only two minutes to make the decision. When Charlotte reached the narrow strip of tarmac that served as the main road, she would have to turn left or right.

To the right, beyond the village, was Casa D'Orio. Olivia stared, impressed, at the brochure with its pictures of imposing stone buildings and the long driveway lined with cedar trees.

"Established for over one hundred years," Olivia read aloud. "How amazing is that? More than a century of winemaking experience is lavished into these multiple-award-winning wines. The passion of the D'Orio family goes back generations and today owner Enzo D'Orio is at the helm. They are the leading wine farm in the area and one of the premier estates in Italy."

"So we're turning right then?" Charlotte asked.

"Wait, wait." Olivia grabbed the other brochure. "La Leggenda was founded in 1969, when two smaller wineries joined into one. The romance between neighboring wine farm owners led to the birth of a legendary estate, and today the farm remains in the loving hands of the Vescovi family. Known for its boutique offering of top quality wines, many of which feature in Michelin-starred restaurants, the winery has gained worldwide fame for its signature red blend."

"That sounds great, too," Charlotte said. "It's your call." She stopped the car at the junction.

Which to choose?

If she could own one of these wine farms, which would it be? Olivia wondered.

Prestige and prizewinning quality were what she dreamed of, but the lure of romance won the day. Imagine starting a wine label as a result of a love affair. That was truly unique.

"Left it is," Olivia decided, and Charlotte turned toward La Leggenda.

Five minutes later, they were heading up the winding driveway, lined with colorful wild roses and geraniums. When the winery came into view, Olivia was charmed by how the rose-gold buildings blended into the landscape, harmonizing with the hilly terrain. The estate was appealing, rather than imposing. It was like arriving at a romantic retreat, she decided, even though as they grew closer, she was impressed by the scale and size of the place.

The parking lot was crammed with vehicles. Carefully, Charlotte squeezed the Fiat into the only available space, under the sprawling branches of an ancient olive tree.

They walked up the paved pathway, through a large oak door which stood wide open, and into the tiled hallway.

"Wow," Olivia said.

She stared at the wooden rafters high above, and took in the display of massive wine barrels on the back wall. To the right was the tasting room, where crowds of tourists were mingling, and beyond that was the estate's restaurant.

They followed the fragrance of wine, and the sound of voices and laughter, into the tasting room, and headed to the long wooden counter.

At the far end of the counter was a dark-haired man. He was seated on a stool, sipping a glass of red wine while he worked his way through a pile of papers.

He glanced up when Olivia looked his way and she found herself blushing. The man looked to be around forty years old, and was incredibly handsome. Deep blue eyes, chiseled jaw, a trace of stubble on his tanned face.

Caught out for staring, she smiled at him, and felt her cheeks redden further when he gave her a quick, warm grin in response.

Charlotte hadn't noticed their exchange. She was waving to get the sommelier's attention.

"*Scusi*, may we do a tasting, please?"

The sallow-faced man in charge of the tasting room looked somber and harassed. He was pouring a bottle of red into tasting glasses for another group of tourists, while two more couples were waiting further down. He turned to her and gave a brief nod.

"We might have to be patient," Olivia said. "It looks like he's the only person on duty."

"I'll try to be," Charlotte said. "But I feel inspired after you read that brochure to me. I'm excited to try their famous blend. Still, I guess we can do some people watching. Oooh."

Her gaze fell on the handsome dark-haired man who'd smiled at Olivia earlier.

"No shortage of great viewing opportunities here," Olivia murmured, stealing another glance at his tousled hair and firm jaw line, and his manicured fingers idly caressing the stem of his wine glass.

Forcing her gaze away from him, she took in the certificates displayed on the wall behind the counter. It looked as if this winery was a winner of top accolades, year after year.

Looking down, she saw a smaller notice taped to the counter—a plain printed piece of paper.

"Assistant Sommelier Required for the Summer Season," it read.

Curious, Olivia read on.

"We are seeking a Passionate and Knowledgeable individual to assist Guests in our busy Tasting Room, 10 a.m. to 5 p.m., Wednesday to Sunday. Position Available Immediately, until End September. Enquire Within."

The weekly salary was stated at the bottom of the advertisement and Olivia was surprised by how generous it was.

For a moment, she wondered what it would be like to take this holiday job, work in this world-renowned winery, assist the public. What an amazing opportunity to learn more about wine, while earning well and becoming part of the local community. If only she had more experience, she might be brave enough to apply.

Olivia nearly fell off her chair as the realization hit her.

What if this advertisement was the sign she'd been looking for?

Not only could the job provide the cash lifeline she needed to stay in Italy, it could also be the first small step in her journey to become a winemaker.

Finally, the sommelier was heading their way.

"What will you choose?" he asked. "You are wanting to do the full tasting menu, or three wines only?"

Olivia took a deep breath. Her heart was pounding at the audacity, the impossibility, of what she'd decided to do.

Her voice came out high and squeaky and her mouth was dry.

"Actually, no," she said. "Neither of those options. I'd like to apply for the position advertised here, to be your assistant sommelier."

"What? You want to do what?" Charlotte turned to Olivia, her eyes wide. "Seriously?"

The sommelier, whose name badge read "Luigi Lupo," stared at her in disbelief.

"I would like to apply." Olivia's palms felt damp. She felt more shocked than either of the others that she'd been brave enough to say the words aloud.

Looking at Luigi's astonished face, Olivia realized her impulse job application would never be accepted. Of course, as an unqualified member of the public, she wasn't the caliber of person they were looking for in such a high-end establishment. Most likely, she'd set herself up for an instant, humiliating rejection.

She braced herself, waiting for the hammer blow to fall.

CHAPTER TWELVE

"You? You want to apply for this job?" Luigi asked Olivia, pointing to the advertisement on the counter. His tone was incredulous, as if he were hoping she'd admit this was all a joke.

Perhaps that was why he hadn't given her an immediate no, Olivia decided. He'd been too flabbergasted to understand she was serious.

"Yes," she stated firmly. "I do."

"But you are an *Americano*, no? A *turista*? What do you know about wine?"

This was a more difficult question, and Olivia gave it frantic thought. She was about to say that she was very passionate and could easily become knowledgeable, but Charlotte was too quick for her.

"She knows a lot. She's excellent at marketing. Do you know, she headed up a huge campaign back in the States for this brand of wine called—"

"No, no." Hastily, Olivia interrupted her. She didn't want the name Valley Wines mentioned. Her association with that trash brand would be a deal breaker.

"It's always been my dream to work in the wine industry. I'm a little short on actual experience, but I'm a quick learner and I love people. I'm in Italy for the summer and I really need a job."

She'd gotten further than she'd expected with the interview. Perhaps she had a chance.

The sommelier looked at her, considering.

"You have worked in this industry before?" he asked.

"Not exactly, no," Olivia admitted.

"You have any formal training in wine tasting?"

"Not as such. Lots of informal experience, though," she said, hoping to lighten the atmosphere, but Luigi remained grim-faced.

Then he turned, took a bottle from the shelf behind her, and poured a bit into one of the crystal tasting glasses.

"Here. Tell me about this wine," he said, and pushed the glass across the counter.

"Well." Olivia picked up the glass and swirled it around, breathing in the aroma. Nervousness clenched at her stomach. She felt as if he'd put her on the spot.

"Well, this is a red wine," she said.

Out of the corner of her eye, she saw the handsome man at the far end of the counter cover his mouth suddenly, as if suppressing a cough.

"Do I get a glass, too?" Charlotte asked. "I don't mind paying for a tasting. But I came here especially to drink these wines and now I'm just watching her."

Wordlessly, the sommelier poured another tasting portion and passed the glass to Charlotte.

"Mmm. Yum. It smells wonderful. So intensely winey," Charlotte said. She drained the glass. "It's amazing. Nectar of the gods."

Luigi's gaze hadn't faltered.

"The flavors, please, signora. Tell me what you identify, and the type of wine that this is."

Olivia took a sip.

Charlotte was right. It was an amazing wine, but she didn't think that would be the right word to use. She felt terrified she'd say the wrong thing. She hadn't had any training in identifying flavors, and would have to rely on a lucky guess.

What had the primary flavor been in the Sangiovese wines she'd seen at the store?

"Cherry," she said, and saw his eyes narrow. She'd scored a hit, but Luigi wanted more.

"What else?" he snapped.

Under such pressure, Olivia felt this was like playing ingredient Bingo. One wrong guess and she'd lose. Perhaps there was another way she could persuade him that she could add value to this tasting room.

"Don't you usually give people a tasting sheet with all the descriptions and suchlike?" Charlotte demanded.

"A sommelier should have the skill to identify the type of wine, and the dominant flavors, without a sheet. Or a label," Luigi said.

"But the whole point is to read the label," Olivia argued. "That tells you the type of wine, so you don't have to guess, and then it tells you what flavors to look out for, so you know what the wine tastes like. That's why they make labels, you know. Why all the bottles aren't just plain."

She thought the handsome man might have put his hand over his mouth again, but she wasn't looking at him. All her attention was on Luigi. How could she convince him that she would be capable to do this job?

"I'm seeing this from the marketing side, because that's my background," she tried. It was her only area of expertise so she had to emphasize it. "To me, it's about the whole experience, that's what people come to a winery for. Everything plays a part, from the ambience to the design of the label, the description, the brand reputation, and the service. Even the story behind the wine is important as every brand needs a story. That's what convinces the consumer to buy. Taste is important, but it only happens after all of these."

Luigi was silent. She didn't know if her impassioned speech had impacted him in the slightest.

"Is it possible to try another wine?" Charlotte asked. "Or even the same one again? I don't mind which. This is a bucket list experience for me."

Luigi reached behind him and took another bottle from the shelf. He part-filled a fresh glass and passed it to her.

"I think I like this even better," Charlotte said. "This has an incredible flavor. Here, Olivia, try it."

Olivia took a sip. Charlotte was right. This was even more delicious than the previous one.

"I think it's a Cabernet Sauvignon," she hazarded. Her nerves were getting to her now, and she felt totally confused.

"This is the Miracolo, the winery's unique, multiple-award-winning blend," Luigi said. "Partly Merlot. The rest of the blend may not be disclosed."

"So there's no Cabernet?" Olivia asked, disappointed, as Luigi shook his head.

"Your blend? We read about that. It's what makes La Leggenda famous," Charlotte said. She reached for the glass and drained it.

Luigi sighed.

"Signora, I do not think you are a suitable candidate for this job, and I am declining your application. Can I invite you to do a tasting as an ordinary guest?"

Disappointment crash-landed in Olivia's stomach.

Even though her decision had been spur-of-the-moment, she'd been excited about it. It felt as if she'd had a glimpse, through a newly discovered door, into a different and promising world.

"I—I guess so," she said. She didn't feel like staying here after her job application had been rejected, but Charlotte deserved the full experience because this was a bucket-list destination for her.

"Wait a minute."

The voice came from the end of the counter.

Olivia turned and stared, incredulous, as the handsome dark-haired man set down his papers and got up from his chair. He walked across to them.

In a deep, accented voice he continued.

"I think this pretty American woman will be the right person for the position. Knowledge is one thing, but one also needs heart, passion,"—he touched a hand to his chest—"and personality. To identify flavors accurately, training is needed, and I am sure this woman will learn fast with the right tuition. More importantly for our tasting counter, she understands the importance of the whole experience. She will add a vivacious element to our winery, and put guests at their ease. So forgive me if I override your decision."

He held out his hand to her.

Feeling as if she were in a dream, hearing Charlotte's amazed gasp behind her, Olivia shook it. She was in total shock, unable to believe any of this was happening.

His grasp was warm and firm. His deep blue eyes were sparkling, and his smile seemed to light up the room, eclipsing Luigi's angry frown.

"What is your name?"

"Olivia Glass," she said faintly.

"Olivia, I am Marcello Vescovi, one of the owners of La Leggenda. It is a pleasure to meet you. Can you start work tomorrow?"

CHAPTER THIRTEEN

When Olivia arrived at La Leggenda the following morning, Marcello was waiting for her at the winery door.

She felt dizzy with excitement to be embarking on her new career. She couldn't believe the outcome of her crazy, spur-of-the-moment application. She was now an employee at one of Italy's top wineries. It felt like a dream come true.

She'd dressed in her smartest clothes, and had taken nearly an hour with her hair and make-up.

For the guests, she told herself. For the guests.

But when Marcello smiled and said, "You look lovely today," she felt the compliment warm her all the way from her toes to her now-glowing forehead.

"We will start with a tour," he said. "I would like you to see every part of our winery, so that you understand what goes into our end product. Not only the passion and knowledge, but the sheer amount of labor and resources."

He walked over to a shiny SUV with the winery's logo on the doors. Olivia climbed in, thrilled that she was going to see how everything worked. She resolved to take in every detail of the experience.

Marcello drove slowly around the winery building, following the paved path, and Olivia gasped in admiration at the puzzle pieces of farmland set into the rolling landscape beyond. She counted more than ten plantations of different shapes and sizes, some in the valleys, and others high on the hillsides. She wondered if each one was dedicated to a different grape varietal. In between the bright patchwork of fields, groves of trees provided a darker contrast, but a surprising amount of the land looked to be growing wild.

"We have two hundred acres of ground here, although less than half is planted with vines," Marcello explained. "In Tuscany, the soil is generally very poor. So, while this area is the third most planted region in Italy, it is all the way down at number eight in terms of production volume. Although the yields are smaller, our wines are renowned for their high quality." He gestured to the landscape. "We farm where we can; where the land allows us to. Each area has unique qualities that support a different type of grape. The rest is used for olive trees, water storage, and tourism. A small part of the land is too mountainous to farm and that is where our goats roam."

Olivia lost concentration for a moment as she watched his left hand. There was definitely no ring there. Of course, that didn't mean anything. Why was she even dwelling on the topic?

"It's hard work, and very seasonal. During peak harvesting times, we work from the time it gets light until it is fully dark." Marcello gestured to the verdant ranks of vines. "Of course, being Italian, our vineyard workers follow the tradition of taking a two-hour break over lunch time. That is our *riposo*, our time to rest, eat, and relax. In busy times, it can be the only opportunity of the day to spend time with family."

"It must be a challenging wife. I mean, life," Olivia said, cringing inwardly at her slip-up.

Marcello nodded solemnly.

"My younger brother Antonio runs the fields. My sister Nadia is the head vintner, responsible for formulating the wines and quality control. We are all— how can I say it?—married."

"Ah," Olivia said, disappointed. Probably, wearing a ring wasn't the accepted norm in Italy.

"Married to the land," Marcello continued. "To our farming. To our way of life. Other people, they see a successful vineyard and believe it is easy. But we know about the long hours, the sacrifices, the constant dedication, the responsibility we have to this creation of ours."

"Of course!" Olivia said.

She felt herself blushing furiously. Why had she been so quick to interpret his words the wrong way? Just because he was an attractive, charming, and possibly single man was no reason for her to lose her mind. She couldn't afford to rebound into the arms of her new employer. She had to get a grip on herself.

"I know what you mean," she said. "My previous job was in advertising and it was extremely hard work, although of course a desk job rather than outdoors.

But I also felt wedded to it, although it turned out to be an abusive relationship so I eventually decided to leave."

Marcello nodded sympathetically.

"I am sorry to hear that. But glad it brought you here. We have been looking for an assistant sommelier for some weeks. Luigi, I now understand, was too exacting in his requirements." Glancing at him, Olivia saw he was frowning, as if he disapproved of how Luigi had approached the hiring process. "He was seeking a replica of himself. Sometimes a different shape completes the pattern. You will bring fresh energy to our tasting room."

"Is Luigi part of your family?"

Marcello shook his head.

"When it comes to valuable skills, we hire the best. Luigi is a top sommelier and an asset to our winery."

Olivia sensed that he was reciting the words, rather than speaking them from his heart. All the same, she was glad that Luigi wasn't related to Marcello.

Marcello slowed the car, leaning out the window to have an animated conversation in Italian with two of the workers tending the vines, which looked healthy and were festooned with dark purple grapes.

"What kind of grapes are these?" she asked.

"In this field, Colorino. They are a juicy grape that adds a beautiful deep color to our red wines," he explained.

Marcello drove on to the next field.

"And here is Antonio himself, tending a young plantation of vines; we are replanting a famous variety of Sangiovese grape here," Marcello observed.

Olivia craned out the window, looking at the steeply sloping field, where ranks of baby vines, encased in blue sleeves, were planted diagonally along the hill. Marcello was right. The soil did look poor and stony. How interesting that low quality soil produced high quality grapes.

"Antonio, meet our new assistant sommelier, Olivia," Marcello called.

"Welcome, Olivia." The lean, dark-haired man gave her a friendly grin.

"Down here is our winery."

The car headed down a steep gravel path to an imposing building. Although it was huge, it fit into the landscape perfectly. Its walls were covered in creepers, and it was surrounded by plantations of pink oleander and wild white roses.

"Here, Nadia works her magic. She is our head vintner, who oversees the winemaking process from the time the grapes are harvested and brought to this building."

Nadia was doing the job Olivia had always dreamed of. What did it take, she wondered, to succeed in this role? Apart from a massive building, an enormous plot of land, a large complement of staff, and millions of dollars invested in equipment and infrastructure?

Those minor details aside, was there any way that she could aspire to this one day, on a smaller and more humble scale?

"What is the most important quality a winemaker can have?" she asked Marcello, as they walked through the doorway, into a small entrance hall and then through another, automated door beyond.

It was much cooler in here and the temperature made Olivia's skin tingle. The rich scent of fermenting grapes permeated the air. She gazed at the shining equipment, the enormous steel vats, the pipes and storage tanks that lined the room.

"That's a good question," Marcello said. "I would say, creativity combined with skill. Nadia has to manage every step of the process, from knowing when to pick the grapes, what yeasts to use, the aging process and duration of the wine, and then, of course, creating the right blend of grapes."

"It sounds demanding," Olivia agreed. She was encouraged to hear that creativity was important. She was a creative person. At least Marcello hadn't said that being organized was important, or she would have worried this could never be the career for her.

"You need to have a feel for the grapes, the growing conditions, the process," he elaborated. "And, of course, tasting. To make top wines, Nadia has to continually drink top wines. She has to know and understand what the opposition is doing," he joked.

Olivia felt even more encouraged. If tasting top wines was a critical skill for a vintner, she might have been born for the job.

"*Salve!*" Marcello called.

A dark-haired woman wearing an olive green work coat, with her long hair tied back, was hurrying toward them.

"Marcello!" She followed this with a burst of rapid Italian. Speaking at top volume, Nadia waved her arms expressively, making desperate gestures as she spoke. Olivia had no idea what she was saying, but from her tone it sounded as if a catastrophe had occurred.

What could it be? Someone seriously injured? A critical piece of equipment broken? Maybe a whole batch of wine had spoiled. She waited with her heart in her mouth to find out more.

Marcello nodded sympathetically as his sister's panicked tirade continued. Some minutes later, when he was able to get a word in edgewise, he replied, speaking rapidly in a soothing tone.

Nadia stared at him belligerently, with her hands on her hips, as if she couldn't work out whether he deserved a smack or a head-butt.

Then the emotion seemed to ebb out of her. She rolled her eyes at him and nodded reluctantly before stomping outside.

Marcello smiled in approval and turned to Olivia.

"Nadia has been having difficulty perfecting one of our signature white blends. It is a complicated process that requires the delicate mixing of several unique cultivars. She is frustrated because two of the terroirs have produced grapes that taste notably different from last year's harvest. Being Nadia, she has told me she will never get it right and that we should close down the vineyard and turn this building into another dairy for the goats."

He laughed. "I advised her to leave it, to go out for a walk and come back with a clear mind. In an hour's time, I do not doubt, she will achieve the correct harmony of flavors perfectly."

"It must be frustrating to be on the verge of perfection and not reach it," Olivia said.

"Exactly," Marcello agreed. "However, we will have to come back another day to do a full tour. Let us wait until Nadia has solved this challenge."

Olivia felt relieved to step out of the chilly air and return to the sunny outdoors. There was no sign of Nadia, but while they were gone, a herd of goats had materialized and was grazing the shrubs that lined the building's southern wall.

Olivia walked up to the nearest one—a small white goat with orange patches, perched on a windowsill, nibbling at a creeper.

"You're pretty," she said. To her surprise, the goat allowed her to rub its head, blinking up at her in a friendly way.

Marcello checked his watch. "We should head back to the tasting room now. We open in an hour's time, and Luigi must train you on the service protocol, and the wines on offer to customers."

They climbed back into the car and headed down the hill to the tasting room.

Walking into what would be her new domain, Olivia felt glad to have Marcello's protective presence beside her. So far, her tour had felt as if she was becoming part of a big, happy family, but Luigi's unsmiling demeanor behind the counter made her start to doubt herself. He didn't look pleased to see her. Not at all.

She remembered the interview she'd had yesterday, and how Marcello had overridden Luigi's decision. There didn't seem to be any love lost between the two men, and she realized that although she had gotten the job, she had most definitely started off on the wrong foot.

"Would you like me to stay with you for the training?" Marcello asked, and she guessed he, too, sensed the frosty atmosphere.

Olivia gathered up her courage. "Thank you, but I'll be fine."

Holding her head high and smiling to conceal her anxiety, she headed over to the counter, hoping she would be able to learn fast enough to please her critical new boss.

CHAPTER FOURTEEN

Olivia followed Luigi nervously through the side door and then through the gap in the wall that led behind the counter. What secrets would he teach her? She hoped she'd be a fast learner. Perhaps she could impress him, or better still, win him over.

Gazing over the counter, she realized this was the first time she was surveying the spectacular tasting room from this side. She guessed the view would soon become familiar, but for now it felt like the most exciting sight of her life.

She glanced behind her at the tasting room's backdrop—an arrangement of barrels stacked against the wall, their wood glowing in the spotlights, with the winery's logo in gold letters above.

Luigi pointed to a door at the side of the wall.

"This leads to the storage room, where the majority of our wines are kept. Inside here, also, is a drawer with the tasting sheets. Come."

Olivia hoped for a full guided tour, but once inside the enormous, cool, semi-dark room, Luigi simply pointed to the closest shelves of wines that were used for the tastings and showed her where the sheets were.

"Everybody fills in a sheet on arrival. The glasses are stored here. People usually purchase their glasses with the tasting, so you rinse them out and package them in a gift box."

Olivia was expecting that she'd have to taste the wines on the sheet in order to talk about them knowledgeably, but Luigi did not seem inclined to do this, or even share very much information.

"Each wine is presented to the guests, together with a description. Read and learn the descriptions," he snapped, and stalked off to the far end of the counter where he began messaging on his phone.

Although the front of the sheet contained only a short paragraph on each wine, there was more detailed information on the back, together with interesting facts about what part of the estate the grapes were grown in, and how the wines were made.

Olivia had a feeling that Luigi was skimping on her training, and might even be planning to set her up for failure. With the information on the tasting sheet, as well as the knowledge she'd picked up from Marcello during her tour, she hoped she'd be able to get by.

She read the sheets intently, but although she tried her best to focus, she couldn't help dreaming of a faraway future when she might welcome guests into her very own boutique winery.

The sound of voices and laughter jerked her out of her dreams. The first guests had arrived. This would be her test.

Luigi moved smoothly forward with a welcoming smile to greet the first group, and Olivia sidled closer, hoping to overhear what he said and how he said it. Before she had a chance, more customers arrived.

She took a deep breath as a flock of butterflies took wing in her stomach. She hoped she'd be able to guide these two women, who looked like a mother and daughter, through their own bucket-list experience.

"Welcome to La Leggenda's tasting room. My name is Olivia. Would you like to experience the full tasting menu, or choose three selected wines from our list?"

The two women glanced at each other, before the older one spoke.

"My daughter and I have come here especially to try your famous red blend. We might even buy a bottle of it, if you sell individual quantities."

"Of course we do." Olivia felt her smile warm as her nerves subsided. Now that she was actually speaking to customers, hearing the enthusiasm in their voices and seeing their delight at being here, she felt filled with confidence. She could do this, she was sure.

"How about three selected wines, with the blend as the third? Then you get a chance to try two others."

"Let's do that. Is it true that this red blend is unique?"

Olivia nodded, glad that they had asked about the red blend, because she'd been captivated by the story on the back of the tasting sheet and remembered it well.

"The wine was created as a result of a mistake. The founders of La Leggenda—a husband and wife team—were battling to create a blend that was different from its competitors, and that would stand out through its excellence and character. While Mr. Vescovi was mixing the wines, he realized he had made a terrible mistake. By confusing three of the vats, he had blended a combination of grapes that went against all accepted winemaking methodology. The batch would be ruined, he thought, and this would be an expensive disaster for their recently expanded winery."

"Really?" the younger woman said. They were both listening intently.

"He ran outside, shouting and screaming in frustration, but before he threw the blend away he decided, on impulse, to taste it. When he did, he realized it was delicious. Illogically, impossibly delicious. So he worked out exactly what he had done and wrote the recipe down, and it became the vineyard's secret asset—a distinctive red blend that is top quality but is still pleasant, delightful drinking."

"This is exciting. I can't wait to try it," the younger woman breathed.

"They called it Miracolo, because that is what it was—a miracle. Many vineyards in the surrounding area have tried to copy it and none have succeeded. The family will never sell the recipe, or ever disclose it." Olivia smiled.

"Isn't that wonderful?" The younger woman clasped her hands. "What a story! A secret recipe? No wonder this wine is so famous."

"They say that there is a story behind every great wine, but this is a particularly good one," Olivia said. "Now, onto our tasting. For the first wine, I recommend our Sauvignon Blanc. In this area, it represents a triumph of winemaking. It contains a unique, grassy aroma that—"

"Herbal aroma!"

The furious, Italian-accented bellow came from behind her and Olivia jumped. She'd forgotten all about Luigi. Clearly, he'd crept over to check up on her.

"Herbal aroma," she amended.

Behind her, she heard a furious hiss that only just reached her ears.

"Grassy? You are *cervello danneggiato*—you have the damage on the brain."

Olivia spun round in consternation, but Luigi had stalked away.

She turned back to her guests, noticing a few more groups arriving. Hopefully, Luigi would be too busy to bully her again.

"Enjoy the Sauvignon Blanc," she said, pouring their tasting portions before hurrying to greet the newcomers.

The gray-haired couple looked surprised when she welcomed them, and Olivia beamed in turn when she heard the man's American accent.

"You're a local! What a pleasant surprise. I'm Trent, and this is my wife, Diane."

"It's so good to hear a familiar voice," his wife agreed. "We're doing the full menu, for sure."

Olivia took a deep breath. This time she was going to do it from memory, without looking down at the artistically printed pages which she placed in front of them.

"Wonderful. The full menu includes three of La Leggenda's award-winning white wines, and five world-renowned red wines. Although the terroir—that's the wine growing terrain—is particularly suited to red grape cultivation, this vineyard is one of the few in the area that has produced top quality white wines for over ten years."

Olivia jumped as Luigi stabbed a finger into her shoulder as he passed by.

"Over eleven years," he hissed, before striding over to the next group of waiting guests.

Olivia glanced round in annoyance, rubbing her shoulder. Busy as he might be, he was still finding the time to pick up on her mistakes. His interruption had put her off her stride and she'd forgotten her next lines. Luckily, Trent and Diane were too absorbed to notice.

"Well, isn't that fascinating?" Diane agreed. "I'm a lover of white wine but I have noticed that there are far more red wines in this area. Red wine gives me a terrible headache if I drink more than a glass."

"And some whites give you a headache," Trent said, as Olivia took two crystal glasses from off the shelf and displayed the first bottle from the tasting menu, the exquisite Sauvignon Blanc.

"White wines don't give me a headache," Diane argued.

Olivia cleared her throat. "So, this classically made Sauvignon Blanc has a complex, layered flavor with a subtle fruitiness and herbal aroma. It's best described as—"

"That wine we picked up at the supermarket did. What was it? Valley White."

Olivia's eyebrows shot up. Hearing that name spoken inside this elite winery felt like heresy.

Standing behind this counter, she felt more embarrassed than ever by her association with this toxic brew.

"That's it! I have no idea what was in that wine. The advertising looked great; that's why I bought it."

Olivia pressed her lips together, struggling to maintain a poker face as Diane continued.

"My hangover the next day was monumental. I didn't dare touch the remainder of the bottle, not even for cooking. I threw it away and Trent, I swear, our kitchen sink unblocked after I poured it down. It was a shock to me. I thought we were going to have to get a plumber in."

Olivia had to stifle a snort of laughter as she imagined what the campaign tagline could have been.

"Valley White Will Cause You Pain, So Use It to Unblock Your Drain."

Composing herself, she continued.

"Fifty percent of the La Leggenda Sauvignon Blanc has been matured in French oak barrels for six months. A small percentage of Semillon is added to the Sauvignon. This results in intriguingly complex flavors that are full of fruit. The notes most people can identify are gooseberry, peach, and grapefruit. Ouch!"

Olivia leaped in the air as Luigi, passing by again, jabbed her in the back with his index finger.

"Passion fruit," he snapped.

"Not grapefruit. Passion fruit," Olivia corrected herself. "These grapes are grown on the coolest slopes of the vineyard. La Leggenda is fortunate to have high-lying areas that suit this type of wine," she concluded, feeing proud at her recall, give or take a few minor details.

Out of the corner of her eye, she saw more guests had arrived. The afternoon rush had started.

"Take some time to appreciate this delightful Sauvignon Blanc, and I'll be back in a moment to tell you all about the Chardonnay," she said. Rushing over to the new arrivals, she checked that Luigi was busy before she welcomed them. She didn't want any more unsolicited jabs in the back.

❧ ❧ ❧

By five-thirty p.m. Olivia was exhausted, but proud that she'd handled her job so well. Every guest she'd served had bought wine, and the American couple had ordered twenty-four bottles. Her final duties were to tidy the tasting area, restock the wineglasses, and clean and polish the counter to a perfect sheen.

Luigi was striding to and fro, checking the fridges and storage cupboards, replenishing the tasting bottles for the following day.

"Put these in the fridge," he told Olivia, indicating the array of bottles he had brought.

"Sure."

She wondered why he seemed so angry. They'd had a great day, hadn't they?

She opened the fridge and bent to stack the bottles in, nearly dropping one as, from behind her, came his outraged shout.

"No, no, no! *Per amor de cielo,*" he shouted in frustration, gesturing toward the sky. "Not like that. You are causing a problem for tomorrow. The bottles of white must go in sequence. Sauvignon Blanc on the left. Then Chardonnay. Then the Leggenda Montagna white blend on the right."

"Oh. OK, I'll fix it."

Rearranging the bottles, she straightened up and gave Luigi what she hoped was a professional smile.

"Why are you laughing?" he snapped. "Do you think it is funny that we work according to an ordered structure here?"

Olivia gaped at him. Where was this aggression coming from? She thought she'd had a great first day.

"Sorry," she said quietly, deciding it was better to defuse the situation. Clearly, Luigi had an oversensitive ego.

He looked taken aback for a moment.

"Learn for next time," he told her in a calmer voice.

Summoning her courage, Olivia decided to ask him a question.

"Luigi, these are all younger bottles. I have been telling customers how they would mature. I wondered, how does the maturation work? What difference does it make?"

"A wine never stays the same. Tannin and acids are the two main factors that allow it to age well. Acids react, oxidation occurs, and flavors mellow and combine. Most well-made wines can age up to five years and be the better for it. Here, look."

He turned and marched to the wine storage room.

Grasping two glasses as he walked in, Luigi chose two bottles of wine—one from a shelf near the front of the large room, and another from further back.

"This is the same classic wine, five years apart. Vintages and winemaking have been extremely consistent, so the main difference is age. Taste this one. Smell it first, smell it," he ordered impatiently as Olivia tilted the glass.

"Now taste. You should pick up that this wine is a little rough in texture, a little astringent in flavor, and the overriding flavor is fruit, as it has not had a chance to mellow."

Olivia nodded. "Yes, I think I understand that."

"Now look at the second. There is a very slight color difference already visible, the wine is brighter. Smell it. Taste it."

"I can taste a difference. It feels smoother and somehow there's a more mellow flavor."

"You should now taste blackcurrant, cedar, and spice."

Olivia had no idea what cedar tasted like but she could taste the other two Luigi mentioned, and did her best to imagine the third.

"I definitely do," she agreed. "And one other thing I wondered—"

Luigi frowned, looking annoyed.

"Any further questions are a waste of my time. Leave now. I need to lock up."

Scurrying outside, Olivia felt tantalized by the knowledge he'd imparted. She wished that Luigi liked her better, because his knowhow on wine was so vast. Imagine if they could have a glass of wine after work every day, and little by little, she could learn more about the whole process, and how it affected the nuances of flavors.

Reluctantly, she abandoned her dream. With this boss, it would never happen, and Olivia was scared to push the boundaries, because what if he fired her?

Thanks to James withholding her bonus and back pay, a dismissal would be a disaster.

Whatever it took, Olivia knew she had to try and work with this unpleasant sommelier, because if she lost this job, the lifeline she needed to stay in Italy would be gone.

CHAPTER FIFTEEN

Bending over, Olivia scrutinized the homemade wine closely, frowning into the fermenter, half filled with their hopes and dreams.

Charlotte peered over her shoulder.

"So, what's your verdict?"

Olivia sighed.

"I'm not sure."

Although she had been working at La Leggenda for a week, she had only tasted the bottled wines. She'd had no opportunity to visit the winemaking building and learn more about wine at the earlier stages of its life.

"Perhaps it needs stirring," she guessed.

"What did we do with that special spoon we bought?" Charlotte asked.

"We used it for the spaghetti. I'm not sure what happened to it after that."

"Here it is!" Charlotte took it out of the bottom drawer. Opening the fermenter, she applied herself to the task. "It smells a bit strange. Is it supposed to smell this way?"

Olivia shook her head, feeling frustrated. The wine did smell strange, but she had no idea why, or how it was supposed to smell. Here was she, working at a top winery, and she couldn't even assess her own basic homemade wine.

Carefully, Charlotte eased the spoon out.

"Oops," she said.

"What?" Olivia bent forward again in concern.

"I've just seen a piece of dried spaghetti on the spoon. Will that be a problem?"

Olivia clutched her forehead. "That was my mistake. It was the day we were out of scouring sponges."

Olivia felt mortified by her carelessness. She was usually a thorough dish-washer, but that one crucial detail had escaped her.

"Well, hopefully it won't take the wine pasta the point of no return," Charlotte quipped.

"I hope so." Olivia laughed at the joke, but inwardly she feared her mistake might have ruined their holiday project.

Olivia had started walking to work, enjoying the half-hour stroll along the quiet roadways and paths. She didn't know which part of the walk she enjoyed more—the section that took her past the wild olive grove, or the stretch of road that was lined with tall, stately cedar trees. The unspoiled scenery lifted her heart. It was only as she reached the winery's main building that it thudded into her shoes again.

What mood would Luigi be in today? What would he find fault with? It was as if the sommelier had the hearing of a bat. Even if he was nowhere in sight, if she pronounced "terroir" as "terrier" or said kiwi fruit by mistake for passion fruit, or put the wrong cork back in the bottle, he broke all land speed records to arrive, angry, loud, and in her space.

As she walked into the tasting room, she was pleased to see Marcello in the hallway. He smiled warmly at her.

"Good morning, Olivia."

"Good morning," she replied.

He looked deep into her eyes and she felt as if her legs had turned to cotton wool.

He does this to everyone, she told herself firmly. That's the kind of person he is. Stop getting all weak-kneed about him.

"I have good reports of you. In our visitors' book, there have been numerous messages of praise for the charming American assistant. Our direct sales for the past week are higher than last year."

"Oh, that's great. Thank you." Olivia felt ten feet taller, and as if she could take on the world, even if it was full of Luigis. She strode proudly into the tasting room, where she put on her name badge and prepared her station for the day.

Then it was time for the first guests to arrive.

Welcome, *salve*, and *buon giorno*," she said to the four Scandinavian tourists. Then she tensed as she felt Luigi's presence behind her. His glare was burning its way into her spine. She could almost feel it drilling a hole.

"Do not forget to tell them about the special," he muttered.

"The special?" Olivia asked, alarmed.

Leaning over her shoulder, Luigi stabbed his finger onto the day's menu.

Olivia saw it contained a new wine, a Special Reserve Sauvignon Blanc.

Why hadn't Luigi said anything about it earlier?

She widened her eyes. The name was Ghiaccio Sulla Montagna. How on earth did you pronounce it?

With no idea at all, Olivia decided to wing it.

"Today we have a special release, the Gee-a-key-o," she began.

"No, no, no!" Behind her, Luigi sounded hysterical with frustration. "That is wrong, wrong, wrong. You are an embarrassment to this winery, and to the entire Italian language!"

One of the watching guests laughed nervously, as if he hoped this outburst might be just a theatrical joke.

"Yaachio," Luigi snapped.

If Olivia hadn't been watching him, she would have thought he'd sneezed.

This was how you pronounced the wine? Like a sneeze?

"The Achoo Sulla Montagna," she tried again.

"No, no! Your incompetence is too huge! I will overtake now."

When he was angry, Luigi's Italian accent became even more pronounced and it took a moment for Olivia to work out what he was saying.

"You will overtake what?" she asked, confused.

"Go, go, go!" He flapped his hands at her, as if shooing away a rogue chicken. "I will deal with these guests. Like the Italian language, they too deserve proper respect." Luigi shouldered himself into her space.

He turned to the group and smiled obsequiously, summoning up his charm.

"The Ghiaccio Sulla Montagna, or Ice on the Mountains, is a limited-edition vintage which was produced when morning frost persisted on our southerly slopes until May. This incredible Sauvignon Blanc has an herbal crispness and a wild, grassy character that we have never before achieved."

Olivia listened carefully to the description before slinking away. She had no idea what she could do to stop this from happening again. Worse still, there was no way she could fight back against the unfairness, but would have to suck it up.

She let out an angry sigh. If only she'd received the money that she'd sold her soul for at JCreative, she'd be able to tell Luigi to go to hell.

While she was standing at the back of the tasting room, Paolo, one of the waiters from the restaurant, rushed in.

With Luigi busy, she hurried across to help.

"Hello, Paolo," she said.

His eyebrows rose and he grinned widely.

"Olivia? You are still here?"

She smiled back, feeling confused.

"Well, yes. I'm here for the summer."

"I heard differently." He dropped his voice to a whisper. "I heard that Luigi was going to fire you. He was bragging to one of the other waiters that you would not see the week out."

Olivia's eyes widened in consternation.

"Seriously?" she asked. "I know he's difficult to work for and seems moody, but why would he do that? Does he think I'm so useless? Just this morning, Marcello told me that I was doing a good job."

Now the waiter smiled.

"Yes, that is what we in the restaurant have heard, too. The talk is that Marcello will not hear of firing you, and in fact, he has taken a liking to you."

Olivia felt emotions colliding inside her. Was it possible to feel cold and warm simultaneously? The chilly undercurrent of fear over Luigi's attempts to get rid of her was meeting a warm tide of happiness that Marcello liked her.

"Well!" she said.

"A customer has ordered the Reserve Falco Volante Premier 2010. I am told there should be just nine bottles left. Can you bring one?" Paolo asked.

"Of course," Olivia said. "I'll hunt one down right away."

She headed to the back room and weaved her way carefully among the racks, scanning the printed lists on the side of each one.

Here it was. She lifted it down, taking extreme care not to touch, or even brush, any other of the venerable wines that lay in this cool, semi-dark, pristine environment.

She headed to the restaurant. Today, the manager was at the front desk. She was an attractive woman with artfully styled tortoiseshell hair. Olivia had seen her in passing, but had not spoken to her before.

"Hello," Olivia greeted her warmly. "You must be Gabriella. I've brought this wine for a customer."

Instead of the reciprocal greeting she'd expected, Gabriella gave her a dagger-like stare.

"This way," she said briefly.

Gabriella headed for the outdoor patio, which was shaded by a network of crisscrossed lathes, with a profusion of vines climbing over them.

The customer, who was dining with a business associate, was not content with his table.

"It is unpleasantly warm out here. It will affect the wine drinking experience."

The man was short and round, dressed in a formal jacket and tie. He spoke with a strong French accent.

"Monsieur," Gabriella cooed. "This is our most sought-after area, which is why we seated you here. Moving will be impossible, as we are full. Can Paolo take your jacket?"

She beckoned the waiter over impatiently and he leaped to action.

"May I, monsieur?"

Olivia couldn't help thinking of a cork coming out of a bottle, as the man popped out of the dark, tightly fitting garment.

"I am sure monsieur will be more comfortable now," Gabriella soothed. "We have obtained the special vintage you requested. I hope it meets your standards."

The man shook his head. "It is unlikely this wine will come close to my standards. Italian wines are little more than peasant wines, at their heart."

Peasant wines? Olivia nearly fell over. This man must be very rich, and clearly wine snobbery was one of the ways he proved it to society at large.

Gabriella's smile remained in place, although it had frozen.

"Monsieur is correct, of course. We hope you will enjoy our humble offering. Here is the sommelier to pour it for you."

Olivia stepped forward and poured a tasting portion into the sparkling crystal glass, admiring its ruby glow in the filtered sunlight.

The customer picked up the glass and swirled the wine around, breathing the bouquet in deeply.

He frowned.

Then he tilted the glass and took a mouthful.

It felt to Olivia as if the restaurant had suddenly fallen quiet. The tension was palpable. She, Gabriella, and Paolo were all holding their breath, leaning forward, watching in anticipation for the moment of truth when this wine enthusiast would deliver his verdict.

His face contorted and his eyes bulged. His cheeks puffed out and his hands gestured, claw-like.

Gabriella gave a small, anxious cry.

Then the French customer leaned forward and spat the mouthful onto the restaurant floor.

It splattered over Gabriella's white shoes and she jumped back hurriedly.

"What a catastrophe!" the short man shouted. "This is entirely unacceptable. You have brought me the wrong wine!"

Olivia exchanged a horrified glance with Paolo as the angry customer ranted.

"I ordered the Merlot. It is the only drinkable red you people make. You have brought me a Cabernet. Rough, unpleasant, bitter. Poorly formulated from substandard grapes."

"Monsieur, monsieur!" Gabriella leaned forward and swiftly grasped the bottle. Just in time, Olivia thought, because the man looked angry enough to fling it onto the floor.

"Yes, you are correct, monsieur. You must have ordered the Falco Impennata, or Soaring Hawk, as that vintage of Merlot was named. You were brought the Falco Volante, or Flying Hawk, which is indeed the brand of Cabernet Sauvignon from the same year."

She turned and glared at Olivia.

Paolo's face was crimson and he was staring at the floor.

Olivia was sure Paolo had made the error, but his stricken expression told her that he would be in serious trouble if he had to take the blame.

"It was my fault," she confessed, and Paolo looked up with a glimmer of hope in his eyes. "I've only worked here a week, and I got confused."

"You allowed an inexperienced sommelier to serve me?" Olivia thought the Frenchman's eyes were going to pop out of his head with rage.

"It is unacceptable. She acted above her station."

The speaker was Luigi, who had joined the fray. Scowling at Olivia briefly, he addressed the client.

"I was not aware of this special order. The restaurant manager was at fault for allowing a junior to serve you, and the assistant sommelier was at fault for not calling me."

Olivia saw to her astonishment that Luigi was now glaring at Gabriella, who was regarding him with hatred in her narrowed eyes. It seemed everyone was fighting with everyone else, and nobody was on the same side. Certainly, nobody was on her side except Paolo, who couldn't say anything for fear of losing his job.

"I think this assistant should be instantly dismissed," the customer snapped.

"We do not usually hire people of such low caliber," Gabriella sneered. "What an insult she is to our noble winery."

"I agree with you. She is an incompetent woman. Hopeless. Useless! I will fire her later, and have the wine deducted from her wages," Luigi shouted. He shoved the bottle into Olivia's hands.

Olivia felt herself snap.

Their treatment of her was completely unacceptable. Going back to the States would be better than working for these bullies.

She turned to Luigi and glared at him.

"You can't fire me, because as of now, I quit," she snapped. "I cannot take a minute more of your abuse. It is pure workplace bullying, and it has been from the start."

Paolo's eyes were wide and Gabriella looked astounded.

"I hope you get what's coming to you sooner rather than later, because you deserve it!" she spat at Luigi. "As for this beautiful wine, go ahead, deduct it from my wages. I'll take it home and drink it myself!"

She spun around and marched out of the winery.

Chapter Sixteen

Half an hour later, Olivia stomped into the villa. She was furious. Furious! How dare Luigi treat her that way, shouting out those insults in a crowded restaurant? It was rude, obnoxious, and unacceptable.

"You're home early," Charlotte called, alerted by the door banging open.

"I quit. It was that, or get fired," Olivia snapped. She placed the wine on the hall table and marched inside.

"You quit?" She heard footsteps on the tiles as Charlotte hurried through. "I'm sorry. It's been building up to this. Luigi was making it impossible for you to carry on."

Charlotte stopped, staring at her in surprise.

"Did they give you that?" she asked incredulously. "What's it doing here?"

Olivia sighed. "No. Long story. I told Luigi to take it off my wages. We can drink it tonight."

But Charlotte was still staring in surprise.

"No, no. I don't mean the wine, Olivia. I mean the goat."

"Goat?" Olivia whirled round in alarm.

A small, orange and white spotted goat stood proudly on the doormat.

Olivia goggled at it. Was she hallucinating? She blinked, but the goat was still there.

"This is the goat I met on my first day of work," she remembered. "She must have followed me. What a time to choose!"

"Go home!" Charlotte chastised the goat, but she stood her ground calmly.

Olivia made a face. "I was so angry, I didn't even notice her. Now I'll have to take her back."

That meant returning to the winery. Not her first choice of destination. She never wanted to set foot in the grounds again.

"Let me get her some water. I think you need to calm down first," Charlotte advised.

Olivia encouraged the goat outside. She jumped straight into a pot of rosemary and started nibbling on the plant.

"Hey! Leave it!" Olivia warned, and the goat sprang nimbly out again.

Olivia rolled her eyes. This goat was a handful. The sooner she was back at the winery, the better.

Charlotte brought a bowl of water and Olivia raided the fridge, finding some carrots in the vegetable drawer. While Olivia was settling her in the kitchen courtyard, Charlotte made coffee.

They drank it at the outside table, watching the goat munch her carrots.

"I think I might have acted recklessly," Olivia said after a while. "I should have asked Marcello to mediate. I played right into Luigi's hands by losing my temper and quitting, because it gave him the outcome he wanted. Plus, this makes two jobs I've walked out of. Two consecutive jobs! In succession!"

"Two," Charlotte agreed sadly.

There was no getting away from that number, Olivia thought. One was excusable, but two was starting to form a pattern.

"I have to fix this character flaw." Olivia refilled her cup, feeling frustrated. "I should have fought for my job. Winemaking is my only other alternative career. I know I still have a lot to learn, but it's where my passion lies."

"Marcello will take you back," Charlotte said. "I think you're where his passion lies."

Olivia felt nervous at the thought of confronting Marcello. It would be less scary to call him and explain, but calling wouldn't get the goat back to the winery.

In any case, difficult topics were better discussed in person.

"I'll take a shower first," she decided, thinking some more about her prospective meeting with Marcello. "And redo my make-up."

"Maybe a low-cut blouse?" Charlotte suggested.

Olivia considered the idea.

"Medium-low would definitely be advisable."

"I'll see if I can fashion a harness for the goat," Charlotte said.

Feeling butterflies in her stomach all over again, Olivia hurried off to get ready.

⚜ ⚜ ⚜

Later in the afternoon, she walked up the winery's winding drive.

She'd thought carefully about what to say. She would plead with Marcello for her sommelier job back. If that didn't work, she would ask if she could transfer to a different department.

That seemed like an adult way to handle things. She hoped Marcello would be impressed by her mature desire to manage the situation.

Charlotte had created a safety harness using her blue gym top and Olivia's leather belt. The goat had trained beautifully to the harness and had walked alongside Olivia slowly, but without showing any desire to stray.

Deciding that animal welfare took priority over job security, Olivia's first stop was the goat dairy at the top of the hill.

"Ah," the manager said when he saw her approach. "You have returned Erba to us. Thank you."

Erba? So this goat had a name?

"She followed me home," Olivia explained, bending down to unfasten the gym top and help the goat step out of it.

The manager nodded. "She is our naughtiest animal. She is a year old and already we know her well as an escape artist and free spirit. Her name, in English, means 'herb.'"

He scratched her affectionately on her head before disappearing into the dairy.

With animal welfare taken care of, that left the job issue.

Olivia swallowed her butterflies down. She switched her walking shoes for the heels she'd packed in her purse, and walked down the hill to see if she could find Marcello.

His office was accessed through the tasting room. That meant she would have to confront Luigi on her way in. Preparing herself for the stand-up fight she knew would commence, Olivia headed inside.

She was relieved that Luigi was nowhere in sight. Two groups of guests were at the counter, impatiently waiting for service. With nervousness churning inside her, she checked Marcello's office, but it was locked up.

As she returned to the tasting room, she saw Nadia hurrying in.

"Hello," Olivia greeted her. "Do you know where Marcello is? His office is closed."

"We have been out the whole afternoon, taking a group on a vineyard tour. We just got back, and he went straight off to a meeting."

Disappointed, Olivia nodded, wondering what she should do now. Should she wait? How long would he be?

"Where is Luigi?" Nadia asked.

"I don't know. I haven't seen him."

"Well, I will have to look for him then."

Gesticulating in annoyance, as if Olivia should have been able to make the sommelier materialize in front of her, Nadia marched into the wine storage room.

"Luigi?" she called.

Olivia's heart skipped a beat as Marcello walked in. Maybe his meeting had been canceled. At any rate, here he was. He looked concerned to see unattended customers in the winery, but his face softened when he saw Olivia.

"I am glad to see you here. I understand there was some trouble this morning?" he asked.

"Yes." Olivia nodded.

"What happened? Can you give me your version?" he asked.

"Of course."

Grateful for the opportunity to explain her side of the story, Olivia took a deep breath.

"It started—" she began.

Then she jumped.

From somewhere inside the storage room, she heard Nadia let out a terrified scream.

Reflexively, Marcello grasped her arm and for a moment Olivia felt as if the warm touch of his fingers was seared there.

Then he sprinted in the direction of the sound, with Olivia following as fast as she could in her high-heeled sandals.

CHAPTER SEVENTEEN

A s Olivia and Marcello ran into the storage room, Nadia screamed again.
"Help me! Somebody! Come quick!"

Nadia stood at the far end of the storage room, beyond the wine shelves, staring down and wringing her hands. Marcello rushed up to his sister, placing his hands protectively on her shoulders.

"Oh, *mio Dio*," he murmured.

Olivia stopped by the shelves, feeling unsure about what to do, watching in growing apprehension as Marcello crossed himself. She noticed, again, the smell of wine—more intense than usual, as if a bottle had spilled.

Dread curdled in Olivia's stomach as she began to suspect what had happened.

She needed to be sure. Her curiosity was stronger than her fear—or more likely, it was her stupidity that was stronger. At any rate, she had a morbid compulsion to see what was there, why Nadia's face was sheet-white, and why Marcello's hands were visibly trembling as he opened his phone.

Tiptoeing around the shelf, she took a look at the scene.

Olivia clapped her hand over her mouth to muffle the terrified squeak that emerged.

Luigi lay on his back. His eyes and mouth were wide open, his arms spread wide. Around him, on the white-tiled floor, lay a giant pool of blood.

Even as Olivia goggled in dismay, she realized it wasn't blood. There was broken glass in it. It was red wine. That was where the smell was coming from, that sharp, rich odor of freshly poured wine.

Nadia was in tears, sobbing, hyperventilating. She stumbled past Olivia, nearly knocking her off her feet.

"I cannot stand to see this. I am in shock. I need air," she said, and staggered blindly out of the storage room. Olivia flinched as she bumped one of the shelves, but although there was an ominous clanking, no bottles fell.

Marcello turned to her, his face drawn with tension.

"Olivia, are you able to help me?"

"Yes, I will try." She wasn't sure if she would be able to, because her heart was pounding and she felt as if she was having an out-of-body experience, but she had to do her best. For him.

"There are guests waiting to do a tasting. We must ask them to leave. Will you be able to handle that for me? The police might want to speak to them at a later stage, so we should take their information."

"Of course I will."

"Thank you." His voice was filled with gratitude.

Olivia felt dizzy with shock. She found herself unable to process what had just happened. She hoped that she could pull herself together enough to reassure the waiting guests, and send them on their way calmly, so that none of them suspected a dead body was lying in the storage room.

A dead body? She'd never seen a dead body before. She was struggling to accept such a thing had actually happened. She had believed, in that first shocked moment, that Marcello would say it was just a concussion, and that Luigi would climb to his feet and probably start ranting at her for causing the mess.

Then her next assumption was that it had occurred through natural causes, but the damning evidence of the broken bottle sent that theory out the window.

She felt relieved to turn away from the macabre scene in the wine storage room. Taking a deep breath and summoning up all the inner Zen she possessed to help her through this difficult moment, Olivia headed back to the tasting room.

There were now four groups of waiting guests, and they looked concerned. She guessed they'd seen Nadia's speedy exit, which had alerted them that something untoward had happened.

Olivia did her best to speak coherently as the guests turned to her in expectation.

"*Buon giorno*," she greeted them in a squeaky, unlevel voice. "I am so sorry, but there has been an unfortunate incident involving one of our staff members."

What else could she say that would be truthful while not damaging the winery's reputation?

"We are going to have to call for medical assistance urgently and will regretfully have to close the tasting room for the day," she said.

Now there were nods. People had stopped looking alarmed. Olivia's explanation had downgraded the likely threat from "potential murder" to "maybe staff member had a heart attack."

"Please can I take your details before you leave, in case we need to be in touch with you again," she added.

She could see it in their widening eyes. The threat had been upgraded once again from "maybe staff member had a heart attack" to "murder, definitely a murder, they want to ask us if we saw anything."

Olivia continued in as professional a tone as she could muster. "Also, so that we may offer you a gift from La Leggenda, to compensate you for the inconvenience today."

Now the guests were looking calmer again. The threat hadn't been downgraded but it had undergone a lateral move, from "definitely a murder" to "definitely a murder, but the winery is going to give us free stuff to make up for it."

"Perhaps you could all write your details in the visitors' book?" Olivia suggested.

She turned to a fresh page, hoping that nobody noticed her hands were shaking so badly she nearly ripped the paper. The visitors formed an orderly line, ready to write down their names, addresses, and contact details.

"What happened?" a teenage girl in shorts and sandals asked Olivia as they waited.

She sensed that everyone was suddenly listening hard.

"I'm not sure myself," Olivia said. "I was just asked to communicate this information to you. The winery will be open as usual tomorrow morning."

She heard a few of the guests let out disappointed sighs that the gory details were not forthcoming.

A few minutes after the last guest had filled in the book and left, the police arrived. Peering out the window, Olivia saw two gray Fiats and a coroner's van pull up in the parking lot. She looked, wide-eyed, at the coroner's van. It felt bizarre, unreal, to see such a vehicle parked outside this winery. She couldn't get it into her head that the quiet, shadowed storage room had become a crime scene.

Marcello strode to the door to meet the police, and a conversation followed in rapid Italian. Olivia retreated to the counter, wondering what he was saying and what the police were asking. The detective in charge was a woman, short and slim, with steel gray hair cut in a bob.

As she watched the group head through to the storage room, Olivia wondered who on earth could have done such a thing. How had this dreadful incident played out?

The bottle couldn't have fallen accidentally, could it? For a moment, Olivia clutched at the thought before reluctantly dismissing it. Luigi hadn't been close enough to the shelves. Someone must have hit him with it. But who?

Olivia guessed that the police would be looking for motives, for people at the winery who had a reason to bludgeon Luigi with a glass bottle. They'd be looking for people with a history of conflict with him, and who'd been on the scene at the time of the murder. She'd noticed a few Fiats when she'd arrived so there had been a number of staff there.

And, of course, herself.

Olivia thought about that some more, with an uneasy feeling in her stomach.

Out of everyone, she'd been working closest with Luigi over the past week and a lot of people had seen how he treated her. Luigi hadn't been shy about shouting at her in front of onlookers, whether they were winery guests or other staff.

Oops, Olivia thought.

Just that morning, she'd publicly announced, in front of witnesses, that she was quitting due to his treatment. In fact, she'd given it quite the send-off and had said—she cringed at her words—she hoped he'd get what was coming to him soon. Everyone would know about that by now. Even Marcello had known.

Oops again, she thought, biting her lip nervously.

She'd come to ask for her job back, but nobody else knew how desperately she needed it, because of James refusing to wire her bonus and back pay.

She'd been at the winery at the time of the murder. Theoretically she could easily have grabbed a bottle, marched into the back room, brained Luigi with it, and calmly returned to the tasting room.

Oops a third and final time, Olivia realized.

There was a quiet throat clearing behind her.

She spun round to see the gray-haired lady detective standing there, watching her impassively.

"Olivia Glass?" she asked. "I am Detective Caputi. Please come to the restaurant. I would like to question you."

"I didn't do it, I promise," Olivia pleaded.

As she followed the detective to the restaurant, Olivia realized that probably hadn't been the most sensible opening line.

It made her sound guilty.

Olivia sat down at the restaurant table where the salt and pepper and place mats had been cleared away, and in their place a notepad and tape recorder were waiting. She realized this was the first time she'd sat down in this renowned gourmet restaurant, and it was to be questioned about a murder.

She supposed that the restaurant bookings would be canceled tonight. The last of the lunch time guests had already left but the evening ones had not yet arrived.

She tried not to fidget nervously while the detective set up her equipment. The gray-haired woman looked organized and methodical. For some reason, Olivia would have preferred her to look disorganized and chaotic. She was scared that relentless logic, remorselessly applied, might lead the police to arrest the most likely suspect. She was appalled to realize at this present time, that was probably her.

After taking her details, Detective Caputi began the interview.

"When and why did you begin working here?"

Olivia gave her what she hoped was a winning smile, but saw no reciprocal warmth in the other woman's dark, piercing eyes.

"I came for a holiday with my friend, and decided to stay longer, so I applied for this job last week so that I'd be able to afford to live here."

"I have heard that you were often in conflict with the victim, Luigi Lupo. Is that correct?"

"He was a difficult person. He fought with everyone." Olivia decided to play her part in casting the net wider. After all, Luigi had definitely been unfriendly toward Gabriella, who ran this restaurant. He didn't even like Marcello. In fact, she'd never seen him be nice to anyone except when he turned on his fake charm for the guests.

"It was tough working for him sometimes. I found it a problem when he shouted in public." Olivia spread her hands. "I mean, that's bad PR, right? It annoys people. I think he annoyed a lot of people. Almost everybody, in fact."

"I was told you had a particular problem with him earlier today."

"Yes, at lunch time he said he was going to fire me, but I quit first." Olivia felt herself redden. This wasn't looking good for her, despite her efforts in enlarging the suspect pool. She felt angry at Luigi all over again. Of course, she was sorry that he was dead, but his unfair treatment had landed her in the hot seat.

"He shouted at me in the middle of a crowded restaurant and I thought— well, I thought maybe, if I can't get it right, it's not the job for me. So yes, I quit before he could fire me, and I decided that just for educational purposes, I would tell him my feelings. You know, so he could think it over, look deep inside himself, maybe try a different approach with the next sommelier. It was like an on-the-spot exit interview. That's how I am." She smiled disarmingly at the detective. "I'm a real talker. I talk my head off. I'm a terrible doer, though. Never get around to action!" she added, more loudly.

"Why did you come back this afternoon?" Sternly, Detective Caputi scribbled a note on her pad.

"It's a long story."

"Explain the story."

Olivia was beginning to fear that Detective Caputi had no affinity for her whatsoever. She thought they would never have been natural friends. Even if they'd been the only two survivors of a shipwreck, they would have spent the time on opposite sides of the desert island, sending their own independent smoke signals.

"Well, you see, I've taken to walking to and from work—I am staying in a villa close by. So, after I quit, I arrived home and I discovered that Erba, she's one of the winery's goats, had followed me. She's an orange and white goat, but quite small. I hadn't even noticed her."

Aware of the detective's incredulous expression, Olivia pressed on.

"I had to return her, which meant coming back here. I decided to look for Marcello and apologize and ask for my job back at the same time. So my friend Charlotte created a harness for the goat, using my leather belt and her blue gym top."

To Olivia's relief, she realized that she had the evidence to support her story in her purse. She removed the garment and held it up for the detective. "Here you go. Exhibit A. You can see it still has some goat hair on it. Those are the white bits," she said proudly.

Olivia sat back in her chair, feeling satisfied with her explanation. Her version had been detailed and logical and she had even supplied hard evidence to support it.

However, she was worried to note that Detective Caputi had not displayed the empathy with her story that she'd expected. She hadn't followed it with any enthusiasm. In fact, from the time Olivia had mentioned the goat, that incredulous expression had not left her face.

She was stunned that the detective seemed to be taking Olivia's every word, and even Olivia herself, with a large pinch of salt.

Suddenly, Olivia felt a stab of real fear.

She was the stranger in town, the new arrival at the winery, the only American among a tight-knit group of Italians. She had absolutely no connections in this country. What would she do if she had to mount a defense to prove her innocence?

Olivia realized with a sense of unreality that this was the second time since she'd arrived in Italy that she needed a lawyer she didn't have.

"At this point, we are still investigating." The detective's gaze drilled into her. "Without a doubt, it is murder, but there is insufficient evidence for us to proceed further. However, we must formally request that you remain in this town until our investigation has concluded, or else we permit you to leave. This request will go on the record."

"I will stay," Olivia agreed in a shaky voice.

She wasn't exactly a suspect, but she had been told not to leave, which made her extremely uneasy.

On the other hand, it also meant she couldn't go back to Chicago even if she wanted to. Deep down, that gave her a weird sense of relief.

❦   ❦   ❦

After Detective Caputi ended the interview, Olivia got up from the table. Her legs felt wobbly. Being questioned for a murder was harrowing, and she was worried by how badly her version had gone down. What if the detective's suspicions about Olivia blinded her to the identity of the real culprit?

She was desperate to get home, pour a large glass of wine, and tell Charlotte about the shocking experience. What she would do after that, she had no idea. She'd have to stay until the investigation was wrapped up, but then what?

There was always the receptionist job back home, if she became really desperate. Her mother's friend might give it to her out of sympathy.

Working in a job that someone had offered as a favor to her mother, which she was hopeless at, while being ten years older than all the other staff, and living at her parents' house again?

Maybe an Italian prison wasn't so bad in comparison.

Wrapped in her thoughts, her head bowed, she walked out into the darkening evening.

"Olivia?"

She jumped. Marcello was waiting for her outside the door. The lanterns at the doorway illuminated his face, the light and shadows emphasizing its strong, chiseled structure.

"I was concerned about you," he said in a low voice. She could hear the stress in his tone. "Are you all right?"

"Well, I think I'm a prime suspect. They have asked me not to leave town." She gave a shaky laugh. "Apart from that, I'm OK, thanks. It's been rather a shock. I came here to return your goat and apologize to you in person, and ask if I could have my job back. I didn't expect to land in this kind of trouble. The goat and I should have stayed at home."

"I am so sorry. It is unfair on you. I know the police have to consider all suspects but Olivia, I myself am certain of your innocence."

There was something about the way he emphasized the "I" that made Olivia think others at La Leggenda might believe differently. They probably all thought she'd done it, and he was just being his usual charming self, but she was too preoccupied to be vulnerable to Marcello's charms at this moment.

Then he stepped closer and his arm brushed hers, and a bolt of electricity shot through her.

OK, so maybe, despite the circumstances, she was still vulnerable to his charms. Perhaps even more vulnerable than she had been before, because he'd just admitted that he believed her version. And more than that, believed in her, personally.

She felt a rush of emotion that was completely inappropriate for the moment.

"I wanted to ask you a favor," Marcello said.

"What?"

"Olivia, you said you came here to ask for your job again. I would like to offer it to you. You have been trained in the wines, you know the vineyard and share our passion. It is our busiest time. We are now without a sommelier and I would like you to take on the role, with my help and guidance."

Olivia nearly toppled off her high heels. This offer was completely unexpected. She stared at him in confusion. Then her mouth opened and she found herself speaking words that she'd never expected to say.

Chapter Eighteen

"No," Olivia said reflexively, shaking her head. "Having my job back, in fact, being in charge of the wine tasting room is a wonderful opportunity, but I can't accept it now, Marcello. There's no way I can."

"Why not?" Marcello asked.

Olivia wished he'd step back a little, so that her hormones could deactivate enough for clearer thought. About eight or ten yards should do it. Maybe twenty or thirty yards, to be safe. Or perhaps he should go all the way out of sight and call her on her phone.

"Well, I guess it's because there's been a murder here. It's making me rethink my life choices. I mean, what if you have a serial killer who preys on sommeliers? I could be next. Nobody knows who did it, and I'm finding the situation really creepy."

Marcello nodded sympathetically. "I appreciate your fears, Olivia, and trust me when I say we all share them. Every one of us feels uneasy at this time, but in the face of tragedy life must go on, and our farm—our passion, our obsession, the destination for so many—must continue too."

Olivia glanced at him doubtfully. His argument was very persuasive, but she was still unsure.

Marcello continued. "Your experience and skills can save us from the disaster of having to close our wine tasting room during the busiest time of year. Olivia, I am not just asking you, but pleading with you. We need you here. I need you."

Marcello needed her? Personally?

Olivia hesitated.

"Can I think it over and tell you tomorrow? At the moment I'm feeling overwhelmed."

"Of course." Marcello sounded relieved. "For now, will you feel safe walking home? Can I offer you a ride?"

Olivia shook her head reluctantly. The offer of Marcello giving her a ride home was tempting, but now was not the time.

"I'll be fine. It's not a long walk, and it will give me some time to think."

When Olivia arrived home, the front door was open and Charlotte was peering out anxiously with a wineglass in her hand.

"I was getting worried. I was about to call to check if you were OK. What happened?"

"You won't believe this," Olivia sighed, glad to be able to offload at last.

"The goat got away? Did she break my gym top?" Charlotte asked anxiously. "How will we ever find her again?"

"The goat is fine. The problem is Luigi. He was murdered," Olivia explained, with tears prickling her eyes.

Charlotte had just taken a sip of wine. On hearing the bombshell, she choked on it.

Forgetting her own personal misery, Olivia grabbed her glass from her and thumped her on the back. As soon as Charlotte could breathe again, she rushed to the bathroom for a handful of Kleenex to mop up the wine that had spattered onto the hallway floor.

"Thank you," Charlotte gasped when she could speak again. "Olivia, this is surreal. How did it happen? Do they know who did it?"

"They have no idea."

Olivia's mind wouldn't let go of the mystery. Who had done it? It seemed impossible that somebody could have gotten away with this heinous crime without being noticed or stopped.

"Let's take a walk to the restaurant down the road," Charlotte suggested. "I know you're upset, and not thinking of food, but you haven't had a bite to eat all day. We can talk about it over pizza and wine."

The tiny pizza restaurant was a short walk from the villa, and Olivia loved it because it was as authentic as could be. There were outside tables in a tiny courtyard, and an inside space where customers were crammed elbow to elbow. The owner was a cheerful woman in her mid-fifties, and her two sons were the waiters and barmen.

On the way in, they passed the restaurant's large vegetable garden. Looking at the tomatoes, glowing ripe and red under the restaurant's outside lights, Olivia could understand why the sauce on these pizzas was like no other she'd ever eaten.

"*Buon giorno,*" the owner welcomed them, and showed them to the only available table in the corner of the crowded room.

Olivia sipped gratefully at her glass of Vernaccia, enjoying the icy coolness and crisp, fruity flavor. Now that she was sitting down, she felt capable of thinking more clearly.

The police might think she was the killer, but she knew she wasn't, and that meant somebody else would be trying to conceal their guilt. What if that person decided to kill her, too, and make it look accidental? That would neatly wrap up the investigation and they would get away scot-free.

"I can't stop thinking about it," she confessed to Charlotte. "I wish I knew who had done it and why. Did Luigi provoke a fight? Was this the result of an old grudge? I feel obsessed by what's happened. If I don't know, I won't feel safe working there again. Right now, I'm thinking it would be more sensible to leave."

"You need to put your own well-being first," Charlotte agreed.

The food arrived and they scrambled to rearrange the table.

With such a shortage of space, Olivia was regretting having ordered a shared salad as well as the pizzas, but it was such a delicious mix of ingredients, including rocket, green beans, shaved Parmesan and red onion. Looking to make room, she moved the salt and pepper to the windowsill.

Her pizza smelled wonderful, with its luscious dollops of melted mozzarella, the rich, concentrated tomato topping and the soft, billowy crust that was crisp and browned underneath.

Despite all the stress of the day, or maybe because of it, she was starving. There was nothing more comforting than pizza, and no better pizzas than the ones at this tiny restaurant.

Olivia decided she could chalk this up as an argument for keeping her job. If she had to return home, she'd never be able to eat here again.

On the other hand, safety was important. Olivia shivered uneasily as she thought about the killer walking free.

She was about to eat her last slice of pizza when she heard a commotion outside. People were shouting, standing up, calling for help. Could a snake have materialized? she wondered.

She craned her neck, peering out the small window.

To her horror, she saw a familiar orange and white face looking back at her.

"It's the goat!" she said, appalled. "Erba must have followed me home again, and now she's found her way to the restaurant! She just ate a bite right out of someone's salad bowl. She's eating the rocket."

Olivia wanted to tear her hair out.

How had she suddenly become so irresistible to goats? She felt like the Pied Piper of the hoofed mammal world.

"We'd better go." Charlotte stood up hastily. "I'll get a takeout box for the rest of our food and pay. In the meantime, you'd better try to corral Erba before she destroys any more Tuscan salad bowls."

Olivia found it difficult to sleep that night. She had no idea what her decision should be. Whenever she closed her eyes she saw Luigi, lying in that pool of red wine. Thinking back on the picture that was seared into her mind, she guessed that his attacker had hit him from behind. The bottle had smashed, and Luigi had then toppled onto his back. He must have been dead before he hit the ground.

Then the attacker had presumably walked out of the storage room. He—or she—must have returned to the tasting room, but it would have been easy to slip through the doorway on the left of the counter, and out of the winery, without being noticed.

That was a scary thought. Olivia might have passed him—or her—as she came in. She tried to remember if anyone had been leaving, but she had been preoccupied by what she should say to Marcello. Beyond the usual Fiats, there were always visitors' cars in the parking, and her eyes had grown used to passing over these as they always changed.

Eventually she fell asleep and dreamed that Luigi was shouting at her as she displayed a wine to a customer.

"That's not how you do it! You *stupido* woman!"

"Luigi, what happened to you? Who killed you?" she asked him anxiously.

"You do not know? You are *ignorante*, hopeless. I am firing you again. Go away! Get out!"

"No! No! Please help me!" Olivia shouted the words in her dream, but as she sat up in bed, heart hammering, she realized her voice had been nothing more than a low mutter. That had been a disturbing nightmare. Was it fair that after making her work life a misery and turning her into a murder suspect, Luigi was now trolling her dreams?

To make sure that she didn't fall back into the nightmare again, Olivia sat up and browsed through her phone.

As she scanned her emails, she saw two new ones had arrived in her inbox.

The first was entitled *Urgent Plan of Action*.

It was from her mother.

Olivia, I have bad news about the receptionist job. They are not prepared to compromise on age, even to help you out, and are insisting on hiring under-twenty-fives. What a mistake they are making, missing out on your maturity! I tried to plead your case. I sent them a recent photo of you, and even attempted to negotiate a lower salary on your behalf, but they remained adamant. However, Edith has told me about a job at her cousin's warehouse. It involves shelf stocking and warehouse maintenance.

Do you have any experience in driving a forklift? Or can I tell them you would be willing to learn?

Shaking her head, Olivia closed the mail. She didn't feel ready to reply to it right now. Perhaps in a day or two. Or, better still, after a few more weeks.

Then she read the next mail, which was from one of the agencies where she'd sent her CV earlier in the week.

Hi Olivia!

We read your resume and are impressed by your credentials. The Valley Wines campaign gives you a phenomenal track record. We have a lovely client who specializes in niche marketing for wine farms, both in terms of products and tourism. They are looking for a campaign manager and I have suggested you. Based on the success of the Valley Wines campaign, they are very excited, and would love to interview you as a priority. They are eager to introduce you to their clients as the person who made Valley Wines famous, and this looks as if it may already be a done deal! Can we set up a time urgently? The job is available from August and the company is in California.

Olivia closed her computer, chewing her lip as she considered her options.

A job in wine farm marketing might play better to her strengths. Perhaps that would be more realistic. It would mean she could still follow her passion, sort of. Plus she could move to California. That would be an exciting change.

This might be the perfect compromise, and a more suitable choice than continuing at La Leggenda. Imagine how pleased her mother would be to hear she was making a sensible choice.

The more she thought about it, the more Olivia realized that this offer had landed in her lap at an opportune time. Even though her heart was begging her otherwise, her head was insisting that she would be a fool not to take it.

CHAPTER NINETEEN

Olivia woke early the next morning, filled with anticipation about the choices that she would be making that day, but worried about the goat.

What had Erba gotten up to in the night? She felt a responsibility toward the animal, and hoped she was still on the premises.

Olivia drew her curtains back and shrieked in surprise.

Erba was perched on her windowsill, staring at her through the glass.

"Well, you've made yourself at home," Olivia observed, her heart still pounding from the unexpected shock of finding an orange and white goat peering in through her own bedroom window.

She showered and dressed and raided the fridge for carrots. Erba seemed to like them, and she was sure the goat needed breakfast.

Olivia made herself a cappuccino and then took her computer outside to the table under the tree. She expected to find the herb bushes denuded, but to her surprise, the plants looked undamaged.

"It seems you have a sprig a day habit. Is that your limit?" she asked Erba.

While Erba crunched her carrots, Olivia reread the mail from the agency.

She closed her eyes, visualizing herself living in a sun-drenched California apartment, working for a company that specialized in wine farm marketing. It was certainly an appealing prospect.

Then she closed her eyes again and visualized herself behind the tasting counter at La Leggenda, displaying the wines to guests as the new head sommelier.

Into her fantasy, Olivia added Nadia calling her to come to the winemaking building and watch while she created a blend. Then she added Marcello, sitting at the side table and sipping a glass of wine, while he watched her in approval.

Olivia's eyes snapped open again and she let out a deep sigh, causing Erba to glance at her in surprise.

Her heart was irresistibly drawn to the winemaking scenario. She made a second coffee while she did some more thinking. This time, she tried to use her brain and not her heart in the logical process.

Then Olivia stood up. Her heart was heavy, but her decision was made.

"Right, Erba," she said. "Let's take you back to the winery and tell Marcello what the verdict is."

Olivia rummaged in her purse for the goat harness, but when she saw the gym top, Erba capered away. Clearly, she hadn't enjoyed being a leashed goat. However, since she'd followed Olivia from the winery, perhaps she'd follow her back again without being led.

Hoping that the goat would be magnetically drawn by an example of calm leadership, she called, "Come, Erba. Heel!" and strode down the driveway.

The patter of hooves on paving behind her told her that Erba was trotting behind her, heeling obediently.

The calm leadership worked perfectly until the moment when Olivia peeled off the road and onto the sandy track that led to the winery's back gate. She heard the scamper of feet behind her and spun round to see Erba departing the narrow strip of tarmac and heading the opposite way.

"Hey, goat! We go left here. Not right. Erba! Come back!"

Oliva waved her arms in frustration. Erba had been obeying the heel command in such copybook style that she'd been daydreaming about a whole new alternative career as a goat trainer.

Now she'd rebelled, and Olivia would have to get her back. She had never been up this winding gravel road before and was starting to panic. The goat could have run anywhere, and clearly knew the terrain very well.

What if she was hiding somewhere?

"Come back! Please, Erba!"

Shouting desperately, Olivia broke into a jog, holding her hat against the tugging breeze that grew stronger as she climbed the hill.

Although she was filled with anxiety about finding the wayward goat, she couldn't help noticing how beautiful her surroundings were. The only sounds, apart from her plaintive cries for Erba, were the buzzing of bees and the song of birds. Grasses, shrubs, and trees in variegated shades of green surrounded her. A cluster of brightly colored butterflies fluttered around an outcrop of wildflowers.

She couldn't keep up her fast pace; the hill was too steep. With a sigh, she dropped back to a walk, telling herself that running would only frighten Erba. Noticing a rosemary bush by the roadside, she picked a sprig, hoping she could use it to lure the goat back.

Olivia climbed higher, encouraged to see the goat's tracks in a patch of sand. Then, ahead of her, she saw Erba's mischievous face peeking around a bend in the road.

"Come back. Bad girl," Olivia chastised her, but she was filled with relief to see the goat.

A sign on a nearby tree caught her eye.

It was a homemade sign, laminated, attached with string. She couldn't understand the Italian, but the writer had been kind enough to provide an English translation below.

"For Sale: Small Farm on 20 Acres. 2-Bed House, some outbuildings. Contact Owner Direct.

Below that was a phone number and the price.

Olivia stared, fascinated.

An old, but ornate, wrought-iron gate stood open and beyond it the gravel driveway curved into the distance. The land was well treed, and herbs, flowers, and bushes sprouted in profusion from the arid ground. She glimpsed the farmhouse in the distance and thought she had never seen anything so beautiful in her life as that small, honey-colored stone building that blended perfectly with its green and gold surroundings.

Imagine waking up every day and looking out through the quaint, wood-framed windows at the breathtaking view over the valley.

She looked again at the price and felt her stomach clench. Translated into dollars, she could almost have afforded this small farm if she'd had the back pay and massive bonus that had been due to her.

Of course, she'd have nothing to live on, and would immediately starve to death, but putting aside that minor fact, what a beautiful place to live.

What an idyllic location to starve to death.

The southerly view was dramatic, with an exquisite tapestry of hills and fields all the way to the valley and beyond. The crest of the hill behind the house would offer protection from the worst of the winter weather.

"If only," Olivia said longingly. "If only."

If only she could stay here forever. If only she could make an offer on this property, and live in this area, and start a small vineyard.

"Unfortunately, Erba, my choice is made," Olivia said sadly. "I could never afford this place, and in any case, common sense must rule the day. Luigi's murder was a sign that my life needs to change direction. I have to go back and work in my chosen career, just like you. You're qualified to be a goat. I'm qualified to be an advertising account manager."

Looking at the left bend in the track, she guessed that it wound down the hillside to join up with the tarred road which would take them straight into the vineyard's front entrance. Perhaps Erba preferred this detour as an alternative scenic route.

The goat was sidling up to her, staring intently at the rosemary in Olivia's hand.

"You can have it when we reach the winery," Olivia said, summoning her inner goat whisperer again.

She turned away from the humble stone farmhouse, set in the wild, green beauty of the hills, and followed the road to the left.

Fifteen minutes later, she was walking up the winery's driveway, feeling sad that this would be the last time she approached this gracious building, rich in history and founded on love. But a sign was a sign, and she had to be sensible.

Walking into the tasting room, Olivia saw that Paolo had been seconded from the restaurant to provide emergency assistance to a group of tourists.

"For starters, you can choose this special release Sauvignon Blanc," he was telling them in an unsure voice, with a nervous smile. "It has abundant grassy and herbal flavors, with an intense aroma of grassy herbs from the frosty mountains. You will enjoy the herbal intensity of this fine, grassy wine from the coldest frost-covered region of La Leggenda, where herbs and grasses grow in intense abundance!"

He glanced at her appealingly.

Steeling herself to abide by her decision, Olivia walked down the corridor to Marcello's office.

As she reached it, her phone rang.

Marcello looked up from his desk, his face expectant, and Olivia hurried to mute the call.

Before she pressed the button, Olivia recognized the caller as Bianca, her ex-assistant from the agency.

Perhaps it would be better to take the call quickly, she decided. After all, it was very early back in the States, and there might be an emergency.

Giving Marcello an apologetic wave, Olivia answered hurriedly.

Bianca sounded breathless.

"I'm so sorry to call you so early. I hope you weren't asleep."

"It's lunch time here in Italy," Olivia explained. She turned and walked back down the corridor toward the tasting room.

"Oh. You're still there? I'm sorry to interrupt your holiday but I thought you'd want to know the bad news."

"Know what?" Olivia frowned uneasily. What had happened? From the tone of Bianca's voice, it was serious.

"It's Valley Wines."

"What about them?"

"Breaking news this morning, hot off the press. Here, I'll read it to you. 'Following a tip-off, officials from the FDA raided the manufacturing premises. They found evidence of numerous unsanitary practices and as a result, have shut down the entire operation.'"

"What?" Olivia gasped, causing one of the tourists to look round in surprise.

She couldn't believe what she was hearing as Bianca continued.

"Inspectors found the vats used to mix the grape juice and the alcohol were rusty, with accumulated residue at the bottom. The alcohol used in the beverages was not of food-grade quality. Two of the flavorants added to the beverages were withdrawn from the market earlier this year and a third was banned by the FDA last year after numerous allergic reactions were reported."

"This is horrific," Olivia muttered. "I can't believe they were breaking so many regulations."

"Rodent control was poorly managed, and the Department found a dead rodent in the mix of grape juice and alcohol in one of the vats. That makes me want to throw up, Olivia. I drank that wine!"

"Me, too." Olivia felt sick. "The rat probably died of his headache," she added.

Bianca managed a weak laugh.

"Probably. Oh, I'd better go. James is on the line."

Hurriedly, she disconnected.

Olivia realized that the Department of Health inspection had not only uncovered the unsanitary practices, but had also publicly exposed the manufacturing processes. It had revealed the fact that this wine was not actually wine at all. There was no way that Valley Wines could recover from this. They were finished. This was the end for them, and they would suffer the wrath of irate customers all over the country.

Olivia felt her face burn with shame as she realized her marketing campaign would go the same way that the company had.

With the wines being withdrawn from the shelves, the campaign would be canned immediately. No longer would it be touted as an example of an astonishingly successful venture. Instead, people would refer to it in hushed voices as "that" campaign—the one that had ensured maximum numbers of Americans drank wine laced with unsanitary additives and flavored with rat.

It was just as well she'd resigned, because after this debacle, James would have fired her immediately.

James would be in a fury. Olivia imagined him, puce-faced, camping out in his office, juggling phone calls and Skype meetings, calling for ads to be pulled and replaced, damage controlling furiously even as he consulted with his legal team.

Right now, every single advertising exec in every major city in the States would be thanking their lucky stars that they hadn't been awarded the contract for the campaign that had ended so disastrously.

With a jolt, Olivia realized that this had also terminated her future career prospects. There was no way that she could work in the industry again. Particularly not for a wine farm agency who was basing their opinion of her on this campaign.

The job offer would be immediately withdrawn, with a hurried and embarrassed apology. She was certain of that.

"You wanted a sign? You have a sign now," Olivia murmured to herself. "This is your sign. Now, are you finally going to take it, and follow your heart, or are you going to keep doing what your mother wants you to do?"

CHAPTER TWENTY

Olivia hurried back to Marcello's office, feeling stunned by the rollercoaster ride that life had treated her to over the past few minutes. She hoped the ride was over now, and there would be no more shocks ahead.

As soon as he saw her, Marcello jumped up from his chair and ushered her inside. He looked nervous, and she was surprised to realize how much her decision meant to him.

"I have thought it over, and even though I'm still worried after the murder, I'm willing to continue working for you," she said, feeling huge relief that Bianca hadn't called her any later.

His face lit up and he grinned at her, his blue eyes sparkling.

"Olivia, I am delighted. And excited, too. Thank you for making your decision in our favor," he said.

"Do you think the police will find out who did it?" she asked anxiously.

"I am certain," Marcello soothed. "Detective Caputi was here earlier today. She spent the whole morning reexamining the scene. She promised me that they will not rest until they find the killer." He paused. "She said she would need to interview you again, too."

Olivia felt uneasy all over again at the direction this investigation was taking. What more could she possibly say in her defense?

At least she'd told the truth. She hadn't made up a story. Perhaps that was why Detective Caputi wanted to confirm her version, to make sure it was consistent. So all she had to do was tell it again, and everything would be fine—wouldn't it?

"You are looking worried," Marcello said, and now she could hear concern in his voice.

Olivia decided it would be better to change the subject. She didn't want Marcello starting to suspect her, too.

Instead, Olivia decided to ask if he would help her take another step in the direction of her dream.

"I was wondering, in between me being a sommelier, whether it might be possible to learn more about winemaking," she continued. "I would love to know more about how it all works, and not just the tasting side. I mean the growing of the grapes, the fermenting, the cellaring, the blending. You see, it's a dream of mine one day to make my own wine. Would you be willing to help me?"

She stared at him anxiously.

There was a short pause and then Marcello gave a decisive nod.

"The answer is yes. We will gladly teach you. We can work out a program to ensure you are exposed to every facet of the business. The more you know, the more of an asset you will be to us, so we will hold nothing back, I promise, apart from those few specific blending recipes which are our proprietary trade secrets. Everything else, we will share."

Now it was Olivia's turn to smile delightedly at him.

"I'll get to work immediately," she said.

She hurried back down the corridor, noticing Paolo's expression of relief as she opened the side door and took her place behind the counter.

Mopping his forehead dramatically, he returned to the restaurant.

Olivia barely had a moment to settle back into her familiar space before Detective Caputi marched into the tasting room.

Olivia flinched at the sight of her, and knew with a sense of foreboding that Caputi had noted her inadvertent reaction.

The police detective walked over to the tasting room counter.

"What time did you return to the winery yesterday?" she asked, without any preliminaries.

With that question, Olivia felt as if she'd been wrong-footed from the start.

She thought she'd left the villa at about four p.m., give or take half an hour, but with redoing her make-up and choosing the right blouse, she had lost track of time. She'd had more important things to worry about, like apologizing to Marcello for her reckless behavior, and leash-training the goat. Did Detective Caputi think anybody could easily escort a small, orange-spotted, independent-minded goat back home? Clearly, she wasn't appreciating how thinly stretched Olivia's responsibilities had been.

"Five p.m.," she said firmly.

That was her final answer. It was an easy number to remember, so if the detective asked her another time, she wouldn't struggle to give the same reply.

Detective Caputi looked down at her notebook, then frowned at Olivia, and Olivia felt her stomach churn.

"Are you sure about that?"

Olivia stared at her in concern. Had somebody else said something different? Was this seemingly innocent question going to land her in a more serious predicament?

"Well, I didn't check the time," she admitted, and as soon as she spoke, she wished she hadn't, because the detective's frown deepened.

"First, you said five p.m. That is an exact time. Now, you say you did not check? Which is it?" Her voice was like a whiplash.

Olivia dithered for a long, panicked moment.

"Definitely in the region of five p.m.," she tried, doing her best to compromise between the two versions that now existed. Then, feeling that she should stand up for herself, she added, "Are you any closer to finding out who did it? Because I've just accepted a new role as head sommelier, and with a murderer walking free, I'm concerned about workplace safety."

The detective's lips tightened and she scribbled in her notebook.

"A promotion to head sommelier, in the victim's place?" she asked in meaningful tones.

She seemed about to say something else, but at that moment, her walkie-talkie crackled.

Detective Caputi turned away—reluctantly, Olivia thought—and hurried out of the winery. She stared after the departing policewoman in consternation, worried that in an innocent attempt to avoid trouble, she'd made everything a hundred times worse for herself.

❧   ❧   ❧

As soon as the detective had left, two groups of guests arrived, and Olivia was thankful that she was able to focus on her new role, and put the encounter with the detective out of her mind.

Even though she was still jittery from the murder, and jumped every time she heard a loud noise, the guests were there for the experience of a lifetime. They didn't know, or care, that Luigi had died less than twenty-four hours ago.

Apart from the third customer of the afternoon, who was an Australian visitor.

"Hello, and welcome to La Leggenda." Olivia smiled.

"Hello!" The tall, blond man looked surprised to see her. "So they've upgraded the sommelier? Good to meet you, love. Did somebody mothball Luigi or was he finally fired for being rude to customers?"

Olivia stared at him, shocked into silence and not sure what to say as the Australian continued.

"I come here every summer, and the only blot on the landscape is that grumpy bastard. Has he gone for good? Please tell me yes. Then my wife will come here with me next time."

"Yes. Yes, he's gone. He won't be back," Olivia confirmed, feeling that she had to say something, but reluctant to break the news of the murder.

As soon as she had poured the Australian guest his first glass, Paolo arrived with a wine request.

"Olivia, I am so glad you are back here. I felt like a fish out of his depth while trying to help. I did not think I was saying the right thing. Even the Italian tourists were looking confused." He squeezed her arm.

"You did great," Olivia reassured him. "But I'm glad to be back, too."

"We have a special order for the 2012 Miracolo red blend. I am told it was an incredibly popular year and there is only one bottle still available."

"One?"

"Yes."

Olivia looked doubtful and she knew that Paolo had sensed her worry.

"Do not worry. This is for a good customer and I will open it myself, as I know him well. He is not a wine snob. He would be happy even if the Cabernet was mistakenly delivered," Paolo reassured her. "Shall I help you look?"

"Thank you," Olivia said gratefully. She guessed Paolo had realized that going into the storage room on her own would feel like heading into the House of Horrors on Halloween night.

With Paolo close behind her, she headed into the huge, dimly lit room, aware that this was her domain now and she needed to get a clear picture of where everything was.

The older vintages were stored all the way at the back. She felt as if she was walking through glue as she approached the shelves, trying not to look closely at the far corner of the room, where silvery fingerprint dust was still visible even though all the spilled wine had been cleaned up.

What had happened in here yesterday? Olivia wondered again. Who had followed the sommelier past these quiet shelves, ready to action their nefarious plan? She wished she could rewind time to the moment when Luigi was killed, and watch as the murderer turned to reveal his—or her—identity.

Shivers prickled her spine at the thought.

Their voices had dropped to hushed whispers.

"It's at the very back," Olivia hissed. "This shelf here."

She felt tense, as if Luigi's spirit was lurking in the gloom, ready to jump out at her with an angry roar.

"It is kind of scary in here, isn't it?" Paolo observed.

"I'm always scared when I come in here, that I'll knock a shelf over and destroy a fortune of wine. But yes, at the moment, it feels extra spooky for different reasons."

They walked down the shelf, scanning the wines.

A sudden metallic clang made Olivia jump.

"Eeek," she shrieked.

"*Scusa, scusa.* That was the wine opener on my belt, banging against the railing," Paolo explained.

"That's OK," Olivia said.

Her foot caught on one of the shelf supports and she tripped and stumbled forward.

"Aaargh!" Paolo shouted, leaping away.

Quickly, Olivia caught her balance, breathing hard.

"I've been up and down this row twice now, but I can't see that bottle," she said. "Are we missing something? Is the label different?"

"No, the label is part of what makes this wine famous. It has had minor updates but never changed," Paolo explained.

"The 2011 bottles end on the righthand side of the second shelf. Then there's a gap at the start of the next row, and then we go straight on to 2013," Olivia puzzled. "Could they have miscounted?"

Paolo shook his head. "Usually the count is accurate."

Olivia sighed in frustration. "Perhaps it got stolen. Or—"

Another thought occurred to her. She stared at that empty space, strategically positioned on the righthand side of the shelving, near the back.

Very close to the corner where she didn't dare to look.

She couldn't help thinking that bottle would have been ideally located if a person had reached out, looking for something to use as a weapon.

Exactly the same thought must have occurred to Paolo because she saw his eyes widen.

"Or else it broke," Olivia suggested in a small voice.

Paolo nodded. "I think perhaps this bottle got broken," he whispered.

They both tried not to look into the corner of the room.

"I am not sure your customer will be able to receive his order," Olivia said.

Paolo backed away.

"I will take the 2013 vintage instead. Please cross it off the list for me. I am sure, in this case, he will understand."

From the counter, Olivia heard an angry shout.

"Paolo, what are you doing? What is taking so long?"

Hurrying back to the tasting room, Olivia saw Gabriella, the restaurant manager, there.

"I do not want you spending time here," Gabriella said to the waiter in a low voice that was perfectly calculated to reach Olivia's ears. "It could be dangerous," she continued, giving Olivia a poisonous glance.

Olivia stared at her in consternation.

"Come away." Gabriella hustled Paolo protectively out of the tasting room. It was the first time Olivia had seen her even pretending to care about the young waiter and she suspected it was all for her benefit.

Clearly, Gabriella thought she had committed the murder.

"There's always one," Olivia said under her breath, as she headed back to the far end of the counter where her customer was ready for his next wine.

After serving him, and dealing with three more guests in quick succession, she rushed to the bathroom for a quick break.

Her route took her past Marcello's office. Inside she heard a man saying, loudly, "Either she goes, Marcello, or I go!"

Olivia wondered who was having the confrontation with the winery owner, and what it was all about. She was sure that Marcello would smooth it over in his usual inimitable style. She guessed that was part of the challenges of owning a winery—dealing with personal clashes between workers.

As she headed into the ladies' restroom, she met Nadia on her way out.

Remembering her conversation with Marcello this morning, Olivia felt glad to have this chance meeting. After all, Nadia was the winemaker, and this was where her knowledge was lacking the most.

"Hello." Olivia smiled. "It's good to see you, Nadia. Can we—"

She was going to ask, can we reschedule for you to show me round the winemaking facility?

She never got the chance.

Nadia stared at her in horror, then leaped back as if Olivia was a tarantula that had materialized in the doorway.

Olivia could see real fear in her wide, panicked eyes.

Slowly, she backed away.

"I—I'm not going to hurt you," Olivia said lamely, feeling ridiculous at uttering the words.

Taking the opportunity, Nadia dashed through the doorway and disappeared at a run.

Olivia stared after her.

It was going to be impossible to receive any education from Nadia. She seemed terrified to be in Olivia's presence.

Frowning at herself in the mirror, Olivia realized that she had a situation here.

Marcello might believe she was innocent, but a lot of others were convinced she was guilty.

Gabriella did.

Nadia did.

With a shock, she realized the person she'd overheard in Marcello's office probably did, too.

In order to continue working here, and learning what she needed to, Olivia was going to have to clear her name. There was only one way she could do that. As dangerous as it might prove, she would have to find out who the real killer was.

Chapter Twenty One

B ack in the tasting room, Olivia realized she had no idea how to start investigating. She didn't have any training at all in that line of work, and she was uncertain if she had natural skill.

She would have to rely on her instincts, and do her best as a self-taught sleuth.

Remembering what it had taken to crush all those grapes and clean the kitchen afterward, Olivia decided it couldn't be a more difficult business than winemaking.

Or a stickier one, she hoped.

She decided she would start by speaking to Paolo, but remembering how aggressive Gabriella had been, she wanted to communicate with him in a way that wouldn't arouse suspicion.

As soon as she had a free moment, she rummaged under the counter for a pen and paper. Tearing a scrap of paper off the page, she wrote a note on it.

"Meet me at 5 p.m. under the big olive tree. We need to talk confidentially."

She folded the note into a tiny wedge of paper.

Heading into the restaurant, she made her way unobtrusively toward Paolo. Discreetly grasping his hand, she pressed the paper into it before turning and walking away.

"What?" he asked, confused. "What is this?"

Olivia stopped in her tracks and turned around, frowning anxiously as he unfolded the paper.

"You want to meet me under the olive tree at five p.m.?" He sounded confused.

"Er—yes," Olivia said. She was beginning to wonder if she'd done this right.

"So we can talk confidentially?"

One of the other waiters looked round in surprise. Olivia's face started getting hot.

"That's right." She resigned herself that this wasn't going to go as planned. Perhaps she wasn't naturally talented at investigation. Then again, Paolo was also not embracing the spirit of the message in the way she'd hoped.

"You mean today?"

"Yes, today."

"The big olive tree outside the tasting room?"

"Yes, that one."

"All right, Olivia," he promised. "I will be there."

Olivia saw Gabriella approaching with a scowl.

"I'd better go."

Crimson-faced, she fled back to the tasting room.

Now that her eyes had been opened to the situation, she started to realize how many people felt the same way. Most of the winemaking staff, perhaps influenced by Nadia's attitude, hurried past her and looked the other way.

She noticed how many one-on-one meetings Marcello was suddenly having in his office, and how many of them ended up with shouted voices, the employee storming out, giving her tasting counter a wide berth.

Olivia feared that her presence here, innocent as it was, had begun to tear apart the close-knit family business, causing rifts between groups of people who had worked harmoniously for years, or even decades. Even though Luigi had been surly and unpleasant, he was still one of them, and she was not.

This presented an additional problem, because it narrowed down the field of prospects she could speak to. If people feared she was the murderer, or felt loyal to Luigi, they wouldn't answer her questions truthfully, or even at all.

Apart from Paolo, who was on her side, who else was still being friendly toward her?

Antonio, Marcello's brother, had smiled at her as he passed through the winery that morning. That must mean he was on Team Olivia, instead of Team Luigi.

Olivia resolved to question him as soon as she had the chance.

Her opportunity came just after lunch, when Antonio walked into the tasting room, wheeling a trolley stacked with boxes.

"Ah, Olivia," he greeted her with a friendly nod. "Here is new stock of our whites, and the Miracolo red blend. Do you know where they go?"

"Yes, I know where they are stored," Olivia said, glad that she'd noticed how Luigi arranged the boxes.

He wheeled the trolley through the doorway, and they were on their own in the privacy of the storage room.

"I am grateful you were able to take over after this terrible incident," Antonio said. "Such a thing has never happened before, in the history of this winery."

"I can see that it's causing problems," Olivia said carefully. "People are afraid. Even I feel uneasy, not knowing what happened or who did this. I've been wondering who would have had a motive. Did anyone have a problem with Luigi?"

She picked up one side of the box and they gently lowered it onto the correct pile.

"Everyone had a problem with Luigi," Antonio said. "He was not a likeable person. His wine knowledge was immense, which is why we hired him, but in terms of personality, I always felt he was a—how do you call it? A liability to our business, that is the word. I know Marcello felt the same although he tried to remain impartial. We discussed it in private on a number of occasions."

"Why was that?"

"Luigi was rude. He had no—what is the English phrase? No percolator."

"No percolator?" Olivia felt puzzled by why this was important. Was Antonio meaning that Luigi was rude because he never made coffee?

Suddenly she realized.

"Ah, you mean no filter. As in, he said whatever he thought."

"That is it, yes. No filter. He was insulting to many people, in a personal way. One day, I found Nadia's assistant vintner, Claudia, in tears after he tasted the Le Estate Chardonnay, which she is responsible for formulating. He had apparently called it a wine made by a beginner, without any brain or judgment."

"How nasty," Olivia agreed.

"The worst of it was that it is a fine wine that has been universally lauded. Luigi knows that, and his palate is accurate. So he deliberately told an untruth in order to hurt her. I believe it wasn't the first time. He was a bully. If he was feeling slighted for any reason, he would take it out on others."

"Was there anybody in particular that he picked on?"

"Apart from you?" Antonio grimaced. "Definitely Claudia. Especially when Nadia was not around, he would make her life a misery. Oh, and there were two vineyard workers that he hated—Ben, who heads up the equipment maintenance, and Danilo, who is in charge of transportation. I think that was a personal issue. They are all from the same small village. Differences go back many years, and they are never fully resolved."

"Was there any recent conflict that you know of?"

Antonio thought carefully.

"No, I would say that the past week or two, things were better. The antagonism seemed less. Perhaps it was because you were his new target. At any rate, I noticed that Luigi seemed distracted, and did not go out of his way to shoot poison arrows at his adversaries."

"I see." Olivia frowned. This gave her additional food for thought.

They lifted the final box off the trolley.

"Thank you for your help," Antonio said. "If you run short of any wines, let me know. They are used up so fast in our busy season."

"I will do," Olivia promised. "Thank you."

She returned to the tasting room feeling confused. Any one of those people, theoretically, could have murdered Luigi in anger. However, the conflict with all of them had lessened over the past week or two, which put the ball firmly back into her court again.

Olivia sighed. The investigation wasn't going as smoothly as she had hoped. If the sharp Detective Caputi questioned the workers and they told her the same thing, she would suspect Olivia more than ever.

There must be another reason why Luigi had been distracted.

The change in his behavior that Antonio had noted was an important piece of information. Perhaps it was the key that could unlock this mystery, if she could find out its cause.

At five p.m. exactly, Olivia headed outside to find Paolo waiting under the olive tree. He had changed out of the white, starched shirt he wore for restaurant service, and was wearing a T-shirt with the ACF Fiorentina football team logo.

"I am off to play soccer with my friends now," he told her, smiling. "What do you need to know?"

"I want to know about Luigi," Olivia said.

"You are looking for reasons why he was killed?" Paolo raised his eyebrows. "I hope you can find out. Everybody is curious, and worried. Some are fearful."

"Someone must have hated him enough to hit him over the head with the bottle of 2012 Miracolo," Olivia agreed. "I want to find out who it was, so that people stop thinking it was me."

"Not everybody working in the restaurant thinks it was you," Paolo said soothingly.

Olivia bit her lip.

"I'd rather nobody did. I need this job and it's difficult to do it properly when everyone's avoiding me, and having meetings with Marcello saying they don't want to work anymore if I stay here."

Paolo nodded.

"Yes, I can see that is difficult."

"I noticed that Luigi seemed to have a problem with Gabriella," Olivia said. "Is there a reason?"

Paolo gave a small, wry smile.

"Well, yes."

"Go on?" Olivia encouraged him, feeling hopeful.

Paolo lowered his voice, sidling next to her.

"Gabriella is Marcello's ex-girlfriend."

"What?" Olivia leaned closer as she absorbed this information.

"They dated for a year or two. She moved in with him for a while. But it didn't work out; it was her fault. As she showed herself to you, that is her true nature. However, by then she was managing the restaurant and Marcello did not wish for her to lose her job. But anyway, after Marcello broke up with Gabriella, she had a brief affair with Luigi," Paolo said in a low voice.

"With Luigi?" Olivia's eyebrows shot up. This was juicier than she'd expected.

"I saw them kissing, out here in the parking lot. Then I started to notice other things, other details. I think she made sure Marcello knew, too. It did not last long and of course, it was for the wrong reasons."

"Rebound?"

"Yes, and to make Marcello jealous."

Olivia felt as if her eyebrows might just reach her hairline. This entire drama was venturing into territory way beyond her imagination.

She tried to visualize what she might do, if she had been dating Marcello and he broke up with her. She got as far as dating him, and found herself getting short of breath. What would happen after that, she didn't dare to think.

"Why did the affair with Luigi end?" she asked, forcing her mind back to the salient points of the conversation.

"Luigi ended it, and he did not do it in a nice way," Paolo confessed in a low voice. "I heard their fight. He mocked her in front of three of the waitresses. He said he knew she had been trying to use him, and he had been doing the same to her."

Olivia's eyes widened. The experience must have been emotionally gutting for Gabriella. Whether or not she'd actually been using Luigi, the old saying "Hell hath no fury like a woman scorned" was surely relevant. Gabriella must have been beside herself with rage.

"When did this all happen?" Olivia asked.

"Marcello broke up with her in December," Paolo said. "The affair with Luigi began in February and ended in early April."

Olivia frowned. She would have preferred a more recent timeline, but then again, maybe Gabriella had been suppressing her feelings, and her anger had built up over the days until it had exploded.

At any rate, Gabriella was now her primary suspect. She had personal experience of how vicious and cruel the restaurant manager could be. A woman who could taunt an innocent assistant sommelier in public would be capable of hitting someone over the head with a bottle of wine hard enough to kill them. Olivia was sure of it.

Gabriella also had no filter, or percolator, as Antonio might call it. She was clearly volatile and erratic. She was exactly the kind of person who would commit this sort of crime, and then angrily deny it, while pointing the finger of blame elsewhere. Olivia could see it happening.

She felt excited that her investigation was already bearing fruit. Now all she had to do was prove the restaurant manager's guilt.

CHAPTER TWENTY TWO

Glancing into the restaurant, Olivia noticed it was empty of customers, and that Gabriella and a few of the evening-shift staff were preparing for the next service.

Before Olivia headed home, she decided to go into the restaurant and ask a few more questions. The sooner Gabriella could be accused of this crime, the better.

She picked up a notepad from the countertop and headed purposefully into the restaurant.

Gabriella was at the reception area, wearing a black jacket, with her streaky hair pinned up, ready for the evening service. She was checking the computer bookings but took time away from this to scowl at Olivia.

"What are you doing here?" she asked.

In her new role, Olivia knew she had every right to be in the restaurant. Gabriella was simply trying to intimidate her. It was a clear sign of guilt, and she felt a thrill of satisfaction that she was getting closer to her goal.

"I've come to check up on stock. I'm doing inventory," she said.

Gabriella opened her mouth as if about to say she wasn't allowed, and then closed it again.

As Olivia walked to the glass-walled wine cellar, Gabriella opened her mouth a second time.

"I don't want you in there unaccompanied," she snapped. "I do not trust you. There has been a murder here."

Seizing the opportunity, Olivia agreed immediately.

"Of course. We all feel afraid at this time. Perhaps you could ask one of the waiters to come in with me?"

Gabriella nodded, and barked out a command to the nearest waitress.

The young girl walked reluctantly into the wine cellar.

As soon as the door was closed, Olivia gave her a winning smile.

"Thank you for being in here with me. It's helping me feel safe. I'm very scared at the moment. My name's Olivia, by the way."

The girl stared at her in surprise, as if she hadn't expected that Olivia would feel scared. Clearly, she, too, had believed her to be the killer.

"I am Anna," she said.

Moving over to the farthest rack of wines, Olivia pretended to count them.

"You know, when something terrible like this happens, don't you find you remember exactly where you were at the time, and what you were doing at the moment you heard the news?" Olivia asked.

"Yes!" Anna nodded eagerly. "That is so true. I remember when I heard about this, I was polishing the glasses. It is a job I do most days, at the start of my shift. I am sure every time I polish them again, I will remember how Jackie—he is the assistant manager—rushed in and told us that we must close up and go home, that there would be no dinner service as there had been a death."

Olivia scribbled down what she'd said. Jackie had rushed in. That left Gabriella unaccounted for. She felt a spark of excitement. Why hadn't the restaurant manager talked to the staff herself?

"Do you know where Gabriella was?" she asked, keeping her voice as neutral as possible.

Anna thought for a moment, staring up at the wood-beamed ceiling.

"She wasn't there. She left for the day, at lunch time. That is why Jackie was in charge."

Disappointment twisted Olivia's stomach. Her prime suspect had an alibi.

"I see," she said in a serious tone, making another meaningless scribble on her notepad as she surveyed the last shelf. "So she was out the whole afternoon?"

"Yes. I can't remember the exact reason. Some product launch she had to attend."

"I guess it's amazing how you remember the details," Olivia said sadly. "Well, I think I'm finished in here. Thank you for keeping me company, Anna. It was lovely to meet you."

"And you." Anna paused before she opened the door. "I thought differently about you before I met you, Olivia. I am glad we have had a chance to speak. It has changed my mind about some things."

Olivia felt a rush of relief. She'd managed to convince one more person that she wasn't guilty of the crime. Although she had reached a temporary dead end in her investigation, at least she'd made an ally who was formerly in Team Luigi.

As she headed out of the restaurant, she wondered suddenly if Gabriella might have planned ahead. She could have created an alibi and sneaked back in to do the deed.

The problem was that Gabriella, like Luigi, and practically everyone else in the winery, drove a Fiat. Olivia racked her brain, but could not recall how many of those cars had been in the parking lot that evening, or whose they were.

Why couldn't the woman have driven an Alfa Romeo or a Ferrari or a Lamborghini?

She sighed. She'd just answered her own question. If you were Italian and you wanted to drive an affordable local brand, it was the Fiat, end of story. At any rate, her exciting theory had fizzled out. Being an investigator was harder she'd thought, but she had to push on.

Thinking hard, Olivia realized there was another angle she could explore this evening, before she left. She shivered at the thought. It would be risky, but it might yield results—if she was brave enough.

Checking the time, Olivia saw it was ten past six, early evening, and the winery was as quiet as it ever was. All the day staff had left, and the restaurant's evening guests would only start arriving in an hour. The tasting room was fully closed—after hours, guests accessed the restaurant from the side door and didn't use the main entrance at all.

Olivia felt goose bumps prickle her spine as she unlocked the storage room and tiptoed inside, heading for Luigi's office which was near the back.

She knew she would be in trouble if she was found snooping in his office after hours, but it was worth the risk, because if she couldn't clear her name, she was going to be forced out of a job. There was no way that Marcello could withstand the tide of complaints from winery staff.

The winery was a big family, and Italians always put family first. Eventually, she was sure, he would give in. After all, as the head of the family, he was the peacekeeper. She was nothing but a dispensable outsider—even though, when she'd looked in his eyes, she'd wondered with a flutter of her stomach if there was potential to become more than that one day.

Thinking of that possibility motivated Olivia all over again. Saving her reputation and her job were important enough, but imagine if, one day, she could go on a proper date with Marcello.

For coffee or wine. Of course, it was more likely to be wine.

Almost not of her own volition, with her heart thumping in her chest, Olivia sneaked through the storage room, edging around the shelves. She couldn't afford to bump one now, when she wasn't supposed to be here at all, still less edging her way toward the closed office door. This had been Luigi's domain, a place she'd never set foot in, and had stood in the doorway if she needed to ask him anything.

Olivia felt her breath coming in gasps as she eased the door open, thankful that it wasn't locked, and turned on the light.

The ceiling lamp shone over the wooden desk, the steel trolley with two bottles of wine on top of it, and the leather-covered chair.

Holding her breath, Olivia moved to the desk. It was tidy, and she remembered it had been the same when Luigi was alive. He hadn't used the office much, as most of his work had been done in the tasting room. Probably, there wasn't a good chance of finding a clue here at all.

Even so, it was the only chance she had.

On top of the desk, there was a metal paperweight shaped like a vine leaf, but there wasn't any paper under it.

She opened the top drawer. There was a notebook, with a few notes jotted in Luigi's cramped and almost unreadable hand. The notes were in Italian and she couldn't understand them, but they didn't seem to be dates, times, or appointments. Rather, they appeared to be personal notes he had made on various wines.

The second drawer contained a box of business cards and a stack of outdated tasting sheets.

That was it. She was out of drawers, and no wiser than she had been when she started checking the room.

Olivia glanced down at the dustbin. Nothing in the small wicker basket, but she saw a scrap of paper lying near it. Perhaps Luigi had missed the dustbin while throwing it away, or else it had fluttered off the desk onto the floor when the door was opened.

She picked it up. It had a series of numbers written on it. Probably the bar code of one of the wines, she guessed. She put it in her purse, wanting to take something with her, so that she didn't have to walk away empty handed.

Just as she was about to leave, Olivia froze.

She heard footsteps outside.

Somebody was walking through the storage room, heading in the direction of Luigi's office.

Her heart accelerated.

This was it. She was going to be discovered here. Her reckless idea would end in disaster.

CHAPTER TWENTY THREE

Olivia didn't dare to breathe as she stretched over to the light switch. As quietly as possible, she turned it off so that the office would be dark, with no telltale glow under the door to attract anyone who passed.

Even so, if they came into the office, there was nowhere she could hide.

Olivia crouched down behind the desk. If somebody glanced inside, they might not see her here. Of course, if they walked around the desk, they would find her in a position that would be awkward to say the least. How would she explain why she was hiding away?

Thinking of the potential embarrassment kept Olivia's mind off the more serious consequences that could occur.

Worst of which was that the killer himself, or herself, might have come back to check the scene and remove any evidence. Her heart jumped into her throat. How exactly had she managed to get herself into such a dangerous situation?

Did she think if the killer found her, they would be pleased, and say, "Oh, thank you, Olivia, how wonderful you're trying to solve this"?

Or would they be angry, which might involve grabbing another wine bottle? They'd done it before and could do it again. There were plenty of the 2013 Miracolos on hand.

She didn't want to have to prove her innocence by becoming the next victim. That would be taking things too far.

The footsteps paused. Then, slowly, they receded.

Olivia let out a slow breath. Her hands were trembling. She didn't think she was cut out to be an investigator. This entire experience had been terrifying. The best thing she could do now would be to get out here and go home, as fast and silently as she could.

The most sensible course of action would be to abandon her crazy investigation, but Olivia didn't know if she was ready to do that yet.

She eased the door open and slipped out, closing it carefully behind her. Then she tiptoed back into the tasting room. As she was heading to the exit, somebody called her name, and she jumped sky-high, her heart shooting into her mouth again.

"Olivia, wait."

It was Marcello.

Her heart didn't slow down, but there were different reasons for her accelerated pulse rate as Marcello walked toward her. He was holding a bottle of wine, which he must have taken from the storage room shelves. Those had been his footsteps inside there, and that was what he had been doing.

"Are you all right?" he asked. "You have had a long day here."

"I—I was checking up that everything was in order for tomorrow," she said. Well, it was partly true. She had been, right up until she started prying into Luigi's office.

"Would you like a glass of wine?" Marcello asked.

Would she? What a question.

"I'd love one," Olivia said.

Marcello smiled. He walked to the counter, pulled out a chair for her, and took two glasses down from the rack.

"Today is the anniversary of the Miracolo wine," he said. Every year, on the same date, I take a bottle from the tasting room, so that I can think again of the blend that made us famous, and what a strange thing coincidence is. I remember that day so well, and I am glad you are here, to enjoy this with me now."

He poured two glasses and Olivia touched her glass to his. The delicate crystal chimed softly.

"Please, tell me about that day. What happened?" she asked. She wanted to hear Marcello speak, and this was an opportunity for her to hear what was in his heart.

She sipped slowly, savoring the incredible flavors, as Marcello continued.

"I was eighteen years old, and studying in the office, when my father rushed inside. He yelled at me to come quickly, and I was so worried I overturned the table as I ran out. I thought there must have been a fire, or that the ceiling in the winemaking room, which I had helped build, had collapsed."

Olivia listened intently.

"He told me to taste and I knew immediately that this was something that could take us to the next level. I do not have Nadia's palate. She is the one who understands flavors the best, but growing up in a winery, I learned quickly what separated good from bad."

"I guess you had the chance to sneak many a bottle," Olivia observed, and Marcello laughed.

"An irresistible temptation to a teenager, yes. The time I took one to school was my biggest mistake. The weight and shape of the bottle meant that the teacher saw as soon as I walked in, what was hidden in my bag. That was a humiliating experience, and my friends never let me live it down."

Now it was Olivia's turn to laugh.

"But tell me, Olivia, how are you enjoying Italy? Are you happy where you are staying?"

For a moment, Olivia was tempted to tell Marcello about the incredible property she had seen for sale, and how she dreamed of living here forever.

She couldn't, of course. She found she couldn't even bear to mention it. It was like confessing to him that she wanted another life, one she knew she could never have.

"I'm loving it," she said. That, at least, she could be honest about. "I feel as if it's home. I never want to leave. And I'm enjoying my job, even though I'm aware that people are upset about me working here now."

Seeing as how the elephant in the room was practically waving his trunk over their table, Olivia didn't see any point in evading the issue.

"It will pass," Marcello reassured her. "This is not the first storm we have weathered here."

What did he mean by that? Olivia wondered. His choice of words seemed strange. Was Marcello taking this murder too lightly, or hinting that she should do the same? If so, why?

He smiled, and Olivia's suspicion dissolved instantly as she noted how the expression warmed his eyes, turning them to a deep sea blue and causing her to become so short of air that she nearly dropped her wineglass.

It was all she could do to stop from spontaneously melting as he leaned toward her and took her hand, squeezing it gently for a moment.

Olivia could focus on nothing except the warm, firm pressure of his fingers on hers.

Was this being friendly or did it mean something more?

She felt it was more, but didn't dare to voice it aloud. Given the complexity of the current situation, she guessed he would be wary of taking it any further. And so should she.

Marcello released her hand. He did it reluctantly, as if he was forcing himself to act with restraint in the circumstances, even though he would rather not. Then he drained his glass and she did likewise.

"Thank you for your company," he said.

"It meant a lot to share this wonderful wine with you," Olivia said.

"It did to me, too. I hope you enjoy your evening."

She floated out of the room on a cloud of happiness. Although her investigation hadn't made much headway, she felt as if her working relationship with Marcello was slowly evolving. She wasn't sure where it was heading, especially given the complicated circumstances. Perhaps it would end up as a good friendship, but if he felt the same way she did, Olivia dreamed that one day, it might become something else.

When Olivia was halfway home, she heard the soft patter of hooves behind her. Loyally trotting along in the dark, Erba was following her back to the villa again.

"What am I going to do with you, goat?" Olivia asked.

The wayward animal seemed to have adopted Olivia, or maybe she just enjoyed overnighting at the villa.

She guessed she'd have to keep returning her in the mornings, and make sure there was a supply of carrots in the fridge, as Erba seemed to enjoy them for breakfast.

Once home, Erba jumped happily onto Olivia's windowsill and began nibbling on a creeper.

Inside, the aroma of roasted chicken filled the house. Charlotte was at the stove, stirring cream into the polenta.

As soon as she saw Olivia, she turned anxiously away from the stove.

"I'm glad you're home, because I'm worried about our wine. Is it supposed to be doing this?"

"Doing what?" Olivia glanced at the fermenter on the kitchen counter.

"It's sort of swollen looking."

Olivia stared more closely. Charlotte was right. The plastic container did appear to be bulging.

"Have you tried opening it? There could be a build-up of gases inside."

"I did, but the lid is jammed. I can't get it off."

"Oh, geez." Olivia thought some more, forcing her mind away from her investigation, and onto the equally pressing topic of their first-ever home vintage.

"We can ask Eduardo to loosen the lid the next time he's here. In the meantime, maybe we should put it outside. Just in case."

Charlotte nodded. "That's a good idea. Just in case."

Olivia picked up the fermenter and carried it carefully to the kitchen door, placing it outside.

Then, while Charlotte dished up the delicious-smelling chicken and polenta, Olivia poured them each a glass of wine from the bottle that she had brought home the previous day.

Olivia raised the glass, delighted to be able to taste such a famous wine.

It smelled amazing, and she picked up the aroma of rich, dark chocolate with a hint of peppercorns. That Frenchman must have been mad not to love it, Olivia thought.

She sipped, enjoying the full, mellow fruitiness, and remembering Luigi's words about the maturity of wine, and how it changed the taste profile. This was a fully mature wine and they were drinking it at its very best. What a treat!

Then she forced her thoughts away from the exquisite wine. If she was going to finish her summer assignment at La Leggenda without sending the winery into a state of war, she needed to find out what had happened in that storage room, and how Luigi had died.

As Olivia ate, her mind was racing. This sleuthing wasn't easy. Was there something she'd forgotten, or wasn't paying enough attention to? She felt as if she was having to juggle ten separate plates, and was about to drop all of them.

From outside came an enormous bang.

Olivia dropped her fork in fright and Charlotte shrieked. Her glass jerked in her hand and wine spilled across the wooden table.

"What on earth was that?" Olivia asked.

They tiptoed to the door and peered out.

"Oh, no!" Olivia stared in dismay.

The lid had exploded off the fermenter, which was lying on its side a few yards away from the door. A sharp smell of rotting fruit filled the air. The tsunami of wine had splashed all over the kitchen yard. Some of it had spattered the kitchen window. The rest had pooled on the ornamental paving.

Erba peeked around the corner, walked over curiously, and began licking up the spilled wine.

Olivia buried her face in her hands.

"How did that happen?" she asked. "Where did we go so wrong?"

Charlotte shook her head, perplexed.

"I thought we followed all the steps correctly. Maybe we guesstimated the yeast?"

"I worked it out through mental arithmetic," Olivia protested.

She knew mental arithmetic wasn't her strong suit, which was why she'd done the math in her head twice.

"How did you calculate it?"

"I calculated that we had just over two gallons of liquid. That was correct, right?"

Charlotte stared at the puddle. "It's hard to tell now. But it seems likely, yes."

"So according to the recipe, I used ten ounces of yeast."

They both paused thoughtfully for a while.

"That seems a little high," Charlotte ventured in a soothing tone. "That would be like building a kitchen bomb, I think. As, in fact, it turned out to be."

Olivia buried her face in her hands.

"It was supposed to be grams. I got confused with all the metric and imperial measurements, between the yeast packets and the recipe. And instead of ten grams, which is about a third of an ounce, I weighed out ten ounces."

No wonder it had created a gas buildup. She let out a frustrated sigh. If she couldn't even make a simple batch of homemade wine, what chance did she have of creating her own label one day?

"Cheer up," Charlotte said, squeezing her shoulders. "Making mistakes is the only way to learn, right? And Erba looks to be enjoying it, so it hasn't gone to waste."

Olivia nodded in reluctant agreement. Turning away from the devastation in the garden, she walked back inside.

"I need to find out who killed Luigi," she said fiercely. "If I can't work at La Leggenda, there's no way I can learn enough. I'll keep on making mistakes. I need expert guidance here. I have to clear my name."

With a sigh, Olivia sat down and sliced into her second helping of chicken. She was beginning to understand why Detective Caputi was so humorless. When an investigation stalled, it leached all the joy out of life. After an intensive day of questioning, her promising leads had fizzled out, and she was no closer to finding out who the murderer was.

"Have you thought about the customers?" Charlotte ventured. "What if he insulted a customer so badly that they reacted violently?"

Olivia decided that Charlotte was right.

She remembered all those guests in the tasting room, waiting for Luigi to help them. If he had ice-cold nerves of steel, the killer might have been one of them, or else he or she could have left earlier. She had the details of the guests who'd been there at the time, and there would be a way to trace earlier arrivals, as every guest completed a tasting form on entry, and many signed the visitors' book.

Luigi could have angered a customer to snapping point, and that person could have followed the sommelier into the storage room. Perhaps Luigi had argued further, or become insulting, and the guest had reacted with violence.

This was a brilliant idea, but she needed to put it into action immediately, because many of the guests were vacationers who could move on at any time. It might already be too late.

CHAPTER TWENTY FOUR

The next morning, excited about her plan of action, Olivia hurried out of the villa half an hour earlier than usual.

Charlotte was in the garden, picking ripe tomatoes off the vine.

"Would you like to walk with me part of the way?" Olivia asked. "Yesterday, I stumbled upon the most beautiful farm for sale, and I'd love to show you."

Olivia felt a thrill of excitement when she remembered that beautiful, high-lying, remote farm. Even though she knew it could never be hers, she felt as if the land was calling to her. She was drawn to it.

"I'd love to see it. It's fun snooping around properties for sale," Charlotte agreed, putting her basket down.

By the time they reached the For Sale notice, both she and Charlotte were out of breath. Erba was setting a brisk pace, and this was a seriously steep hill. She'd been so intent on catching up with the goat last time that she hadn't noticed how much her legs had been burning by the time they reached the top.

"Here it is," she gasped in relief as she saw the notice ahead. "It's this farm."

Charlotte leaned against the tree, puffing for breath.

"It's a nice size," she said, looking at the notice. "What's it like? Is it neat, or dilapidated?"

"I didn't go in the last time," Olivia confessed. "I was too busy trying to catch Erba."

She looked at the wrought iron gate. The small stone house in the distance seemed to invite her in.

"I guess it couldn't hurt to have a look?" she ventured. "It seems unoccupied. And it is for sale."

"Let's go," Charlotte decided.

The gate was closed, but not locked. The hinges screamed when she opened the gate, and wailed when she closed it again behind them.

They headed up to the farmhouse in reverent, and slightly breathless, silence.

The wild garden was riotous with color. Tall grasses and wildflowers were swaying in the breeze. Olivia saw that the buildings were in good condition. Despite being unoccupied, they were not neglected. With windows cleaned and creepers trimmed, the house would be ready for its new owner.

"Hey, look at that big old barn over there. That's impressive," Charlotte said.

Olivia walked over to take a look. It was solid and well built, with high stone walls, and the building's shade was pleasantly cool.

"You see, this could be a wine manufacturing room," she said. "It's the right size."

"Well, yes, but I don't think this place could be a winery," Charlotte said.

"Why's that?"

"Because, don't you need soil to grow grapes? I don't see any soil outside of the garden, only stone."

Olivia frowned.

"Maybe there's soil under the stones?"

"Could be. Just—very hard soil. Immature soil."

"What do you mean, immature soil?"

"I mean rock. Rock that will erode into soil over the next ten thousand years."

"Oh, come on!" Olivia laughed.

"Look, you're a patient person. But patience for ten thousand years? I don't think so! Oh, hey. Hello, kitty."

Olivia looked in the direction Charlotte was pointing. A small black and white cat was trotting across the pathway.

Sensing them, it froze, glancing warily in their direction.

"Here, kitty!" Olivia called.

Slowly, wiggling her fingers invitingly, Olivia bent down and crept forward.

The cat's stare widened and its body language tensed.

As Olivia extended her hand, the cat turned and darted away, disappearing into the undergrowth.

"I don't think that cat's domestic. It might be a feral. Perhaps it hunts here," Charlotte said.

Olivia nodded. "It looked thin."

"I'll bring some leftover chicken for it later," Charlotte said.

Olivia couldn't get the picture out of her mind of this humble, overgrown farm bursting with new life and energy as a functional winery. She could almost see the large, wooden doors that would need to be installed to fit the gap in the barn wall. Rough and rustic, thick and solid, shutting out the heat and the sun so that the interior was cool and clean.

Olivia added to her picture a small black and white cat, lounging contentedly in a basket outside the door.

After a moment's hesitation, she included an orange-dappled goat, perched on all fours on one of the windowsills.

She knew that her visualization had already exceeded the boundaries of possibility. Forcing herself to focus on her current reality and her important investigation, she headed back to the road.

Olivia's walking pace matched the speed of her thoughts, and she arrived at the winery in record time, with the beginnings of a workable plan in her mind. It was a logical and sensible plan, which she thought would succeed. The only issue was that it required Marcello's approval, and she had no idea whether he would agree.

As she walked down the hill to the tasting room, Olivia saw two of the workers change direction to avoid her. She felt a surge of irritation, and was tempted to shout angrily at them and ask them what the hell they thought they were doing.

Of course, that would only cement her position as a murderous madwoman. Any loss of control would have that effect. She forced herself to keep walking calmly toward the building, even though her fists were clenched at her sides.

In the tasting room, Olivia stopped, feeling herself go pale with shock.

Marcello was coming out of the storage room, accompanied by Detective Caputi.

Had they found out she was snooping yesterday evening? She felt herself wilting under the detective's assessing stare.

"The interviews this morning were very promising. I will update you once we have collated all the evidence," the detective said to Marcello. "Further questioning will be necessary," she added, and gazed meaningfully at Olivia.

Olivia felt as if she were in an elevator that was descending too fast. The purpose in the detective's words was clear. Who had she been interviewing and what had they said? What did this mean for her?

She knew she had to move quickly, because she didn't have much time. The net was closing, and in a day or two, she feared she would either be jobless or in jail.

Olivia wasn't sure which would be worse. Undoubtedly, jail would be more serious. But imagining the regret in Marcello's eyes as he gave her notice, and thinking of all the might-have-beens—well, that made Olivia want to burst into tears.

As soon as the detective had left, she approached Marcello.

"I have had an idea," she told him. "On the evening Luigi was killed, I took the details of the guests who were waiting, and said we'd send them a gift. Why don't we invite them back here this evening, to taste some wines and receive a complimentary bottle? We could even invite the groups who were here earlier, in case they weren't able to finish their tasting."

Marcello's face softened and she saw some of his tension disappear.

"An excellent idea. I agree we should do it now, before any holidaymakers leave the area. Thank you for suggesting it. Your advice is very welcome, since I have been distracted."

"I'll organize it if you like," Olivia said.

"We can provide snacks, too," Marcello added. "I will speak to Gabriella now. Please let me have the numbers of guests as soon as possible."

"Can you make sure we have some gluten-free snacks in the spread?" Olivia asked in anxious tones. From the launches she'd organized in Chicago, she knew how fussy people could be.

Marcello looked startled. "Of course," he agreed cautiously.

"And vegan. Vegans get very upset if there isn't anything for them. We must have at least one vegetarian and vegan option."

Marcello nodded. Olivia had the sense he was trying to stop from smiling.

"Any other food choices?" he asked gravely.

"We need to make sure any dishes with peanuts are clearly marked as such," Olivia said.

Marcello counted on his fingers. "Gluten-free, vegan, vegetarian, and peanuts specified."

"That's it!" Olivia smiled. "Then everyone should be happy."

With hope surging inside her, she started her task. There were two sources of data. The first was the visitors' book, and the second was the forms filled in by the tasting room guests. A full tasting usually took forty-five minutes, so to be safe, she decided to go back to three p.m. and invite everyone who had arrived from that time onward.

Olivia collated the information, wishing she'd thought to bring her computer with her. Instead, she drew up a spreadsheet by hand, listing the names of every guest she could find, and all their available information.

Working frantically, within the next hour she had invited back the sixteen groups of guests who had been at the winery during the specified timeframe.

Almost immediately, the RSVPs started pouring in. It seemed that the offer of free wine paired with food from the famous restaurant was irresistible. Olivia hoped it would be so for the killer as well.

Only one group declined the invite, saying that they had already left the area.

Still in sleuthing mode, Olivia checked up on who they were. They were a group of three retired ladies from England, who had arrived at the restaurant for lunch and decided to taste wine afterward.

Olivia didn't think they were likely suspects, but she emailed them back and asked for their delivery address, and their choice of wine, so she could send them a gift instead.

As for the rest of the guests, she would have to hope that her budding detective's instincts were able to single out the guilty party.

The day flew by, and Olivia spent the afternoon feverishly preparing for the event in between serving guests. Antonio organized for a big table to be brought in for the snacks, and she chose some of the estate's most popular vintages to display along the tasting counter.

The setup looked magnificent.

Guests were due to arrive from six p.m. onward. At five, when Olivia closed the tasting room and rushed to the bathroom to redo her hair and make-up, she realized that there was a fatal flaw in her plans.

She stared at her reflection in consternation.

She was the only person who knew the real purpose of this gathering. However, as the hostess, she would be run off her feet serving people and would have to maintain a professional demeanor. There was no way she could socialize with guests on a personal level, and with Marcello also in attendance, she couldn't ask the probing questions she would need to.

Olivia groaned in dismay. She'd organized the perfect setup, and it had all been for nothing.

Her carefully thought out scheme lay in ruins.

CHAPTER TWENTY FIVE

"Think," Olivia hissed at her reflection. "Don't just look at me with that blank stare! Use your brain." She tapped her head meaningfully.

Behind her, the slam of the bathroom door and rapidly retreating footsteps told her that somebody had departed in a hurry when they saw her. Well, seeing she already had a reputation as a killer, speaking to herself in mirrors like a madwoman couldn't do any more damage.

Besides, she had the spark of an idea. What she needed for this event was an accomplice, or rather, a co-investigator.

An undercover agent. That was the term she'd been looking for. Luckily, Olivia had the perfect person in mind.

She headed back to the tasting room where Marcello was supervising the layout of the snacks.

"Can I ask you a favor?" she said.

"Of course." Marcello turned to her, holding a plate of mozzarella and pesto crostini with a handwritten label attached to it: "Vegetarian, May Contain Nuts."

"My friend Charlotte has offered to come and help us tonight. She adores the winery and she's an excellent hostess. She asked if you would give permission."

"Permission?" Marcello's eyebrows rose as he placed the anchovy bruschetta and the mini mushroom pizzas on the table. "There is no need. As an employee, you are family, and your friend, too. She is warmly invited to join us."

"Oh, thank you. I'll just call her and let her know."

Olivia hurried outside, hoping that Charlotte would agree to her hastily contrived scheme.

"I need your help urgently," she said when Charlotte picked up.

"Sure." Charlotte sounded surprised. "Is the goat misbehaving again, or what's the issue?"

"Again? What do you mean? Erba is behaving perfectly, as always. No, it's a different issue. We have a function here tonight, and I need your help as an undercover agent."

"An agent?" Charlotte sounded excited.

"All the winery guests who were at La Leggenda around the time Luigi was killed, are arriving in the next half-hour for some wine and snacks, and a free gift."

Charlotte picked up the plan immediately.

"Aha. So you want me to mingle and ask innocent questions?"

"Yes, exactly."

"I can do that. I'll put them at their ease. I'm very good at that." Charlotte paused. "What's the code?"

"Um," Olivia thought quickly. She hadn't devised a code or even thought it would be necessary. Of course, now, she saw that it would be. "Shall we say 'Red'? If you say the word 'Red' loudly, will that work?"

There was a surprised silence.

"I'm sure it will," Charlotte said. "However, I was actually referring to the dress code."

"Oh, sorry. Smart-casual," Olivia replied.

"Perfect. See you in thirty."

The sound of voices and laughter filled the tasting room, and the savory aroma of the hot snacks was overlaid by the fragrance of wine.

Sixteen group invitations had resulted in the arrival of nearly forty guests. Although they had all been told about the circumstances, the atmosphere was cheerful.

Olivia was rushed off her feet, as she'd expected, filling wine glasses with a selection of the most popular reds and whites, and offering them to guests. It was slow work, because she discovered everyone wanted to know all about the different wines before choosing their glass.

Marcello was circulating with trays of food, delivering his trademark charm together with the snacks.

"Welcome, signoras," he greeted a group of four women. "Thank you for the pleasure of your company tonight. Please, have a bite. In my right hand, we have tomato, watermelon, and basil skewers, which are vegan, without gluten, and peanut free. In my left, you may enjoy our restaurant's slow-cooked meatballs, which contain a little gluten."

Olivia was impressed by the way that Charlotte was innocently mingling with the guests. She didn't think Marcello was suspicious of her presence.

Moving closer, she listened.

"They say good comes out of bad eventually. Do you agree?" Charlotte asked a German couple, sipping on the glass of the red blend she'd chosen.

"How do you mean?" the husband asked.

"Well, such a tragic event took place here. And yet, it has brought us together under one roof, a united group of wine-loving nations." She gestured dramatically with her left hand. "Like a dreadful wildfire tearing across the prairie, and then after the devastation, you see the shoots of green starting to grow, and flowers peeping through."

The wife raised her eyebrows, seeming impressed.

The husband nodded. "An interesting comparison. We did not know anything about it, as we left quite soon after arrival. We filled in a tasting form, but when the sommelier was nowhere to be seen, we went to Casa D'Orio. I didn't think this could be better, but the red blend here is exceptional."

"The blend is unlike anything we tasted at Casa D'Orio, although their Cabernet was superb" his wife agreed.

Charlotte winked at Olivia, who mentally crossed the German couple off her list of suspects. Having not met Luigi at all, they were certainly innocent.

Olivia returned to the counter to put down empty glasses and refill fresh ones, listening to the next conversation playing out behind her.

"I see you're drinking my favorite," Charlotte commented to the next guest, a tall balding man who had arrived on his own.

"The famous blend?" The man sounded as if he was from New Zealand or South Africa, Olivia couldn't tell exactly which.

"Isn't it scrumptious?" Charlotte grinned up at him.

"It is one of a kind. One of my businesses back in South Africa is an online wine store, and I've spent many hours tasting top international wines to add to our portfolio. This is without a doubt one of the best there is."

"You must have been glad to come back this evening, and get the opportunity to experience it," Charlotte agreed.

"I tried it already during the tasting. I tried to discuss it with the sommelier, but he was extremely rude."

Olivia's ears pricked up. Pouring the Sauvignon Blanc into glasses, she listened intently to the conversation playing out behind her.

"Really?" Charlotte sounded shocked. "He was?"

"Yes. I said that the balance of tannins was good, but would improve further in the next five years. He started shouting at me as if I had no right to offer an opinion. He called me an ignorant Australian." The man sounded affronted. "An Australian? I ask you. I told him if his nose for wine was as bad as his ear for accents, he shouldn't be in the job at all."

"What happened then?" Charlotte sounded as if she was drinking in every word. Olivia could imagine her staring up at him wide-eyed, fluttering her eyelashes.

"Then he became so angry he just about choked. He told me I was the worst customer he'd ever served and that I didn't deserve any of the wines on his tasting menu. He suggested to me that I go and drown myself in a vat of Valley Wine."

Olivia's hand jerked and a splash of the Sauvignon Blanc spilled onto the table.

The man continued, sounding angry. "I personally don't feel it's right to insult another winery. It's rude and unprofessional and he was picking a fight by doing it. Every wine has a place in the market, even the affordable ones. Valley Wines was easy drinking, and a lot of folk liked it. I didn't think it was too bad—well, not until yesterday, when I read that there were dead rats in the storage tankers. Anyway when I tried to get my point across, he took all the glasses off the counter. He said he refused to serve me and I must leave. He turned and walked into the back room. Then I—"

Olivia listened, transfixed, not wanting to miss a word. She felt as if she was on the verge of a major breakthrough. This was going to be the moment that decided the case, she felt sure of it.

Why, though, had he stopped speaking? Had he realized too late that he'd said too much? Or was he whispering his confession?

At that moment she heard the distinctive tune of Charlotte's cell phone.

Quickly transferring the glasses to the tray, she turned round and surveyed the scene.

Disappointment crushed her like a lead weight.

The South African man was standing on his own, frowning down at his empty glass.

Charlotte was gone.

Chapter Twenty Six

What had happened? Olivia wondered. The setup had been working perfectly, and then Charlotte had vanished. Where had she gone so suddenly? She hadn't used a code word or tried to alert Olivia in any way. Had the phone call interrupted her line of questioning?

Hastily, Olivia walked over to the South African suspect. Perhaps he would continue the conversation with her.

"Can I offer you another glass?" she asked, smiling.

He gave a curt shake of his head, as if she was a perfect stranger who hadn't just been listening in to his conversation and getting personally involved.

Well, of course he thought that, Olivia reminded herself. It was up to her to ingratiate herself with him so that he opened up to her, just like he'd been doing to Charlotte.

"I must be getting home now," he said.

Olivia began to panic. Her prime suspect was going to leave.

"What about your free bottle of wine? Have you chosen it?"

He hesitated and she escorted him to the counter.

"I think I heard you say, while I was passing, that the sommelier was rude to you," she said as he deliberated over his selection. "Did you leave immediately afterward?"

Or had he been angry enough to stay and wait for a moment when nobody was watching, and then slip through the side door and follow Luigi?

He considered her question, and Olivia held her breath in anticipation. It looked as if her intervention had worked and he was going to continue with his story. Then he sighed, as if mentally dismissing an unpleasant thought.

"What's this one like?" he asked, picking up the white blend.

Bravely trying to conceal her disappointment, Olivia gave him a professional smile.

"Highly recommended. Connoisseurs of white wine in particular love its balance, which gives intriguing complexity of flavors with an underlying fragrant and fruity character."

He nodded.

"I'll take that, then. Sounds good."

Olivia wrapped the bottle in tissue paper, hoping that she'd be able to strike up a conversation with him while she did this, but to her frustration his phone rang and he spent the entire time talking about business.

Then he strode out.

"Aargh," Olivia groaned.

Her best suspect—well, actually, her only suspect—had just left without disclosing what had happened after Luigi's outburst.

Where had Charlotte gone?

Perhaps she had received a call from work, and had gone outside to take it. If so, she should be back any moment. Olivia continued serving the guests and wrapping the bottles for the people who were ready to leave. She kept glancing over to the entrance door, waiting hopefully for Charlotte to return.

Half an hour later, when the last guests had chosen their wine, there was still no sign of Charlotte. When Olivia locked up and walked outside, she saw her car had gone.

Charlotte must have headed home. She was working remotely, so perhaps she'd had to send something through to the office urgently.

It was a beautiful evening, perfect for a walk, and she knew when she reached the top of the hill, she'd have a magnificent view of the setting sun.

"Come, Erba," she called.

Olivia felt a thrill of accomplishment when Erba appeared, seemingly from nowhere, and trotted loyally behind her out of the winery. She was a natural at this goat training game. If only there was a higher demand for trained goats.

"Erba, we could start a school," she told the goat, who looked up at her trustingly before detouring to the sidewalk to eat a small geranium plant.

"We could do group and individual lessons," she elaborated on her plan, following the route up the hill that had now become her preferred way home.

"Maybe you could even become a therapy goat. I think you'd make an excellent therapy goat. You always make me laugh, and feel better about things."

Erba's preferred route took her up the hill and past the farm for sale. Remembering that training was a give and take process, and that a happy goat was an obedient goat, Olivia allowed her to take the detour.

Walking past the beautiful property, Olivia couldn't help but stop and admire it again.

There was no way she could afford this farm, ever. It was an unachievable dream, and it was painful to think that someone, at some stage, would realize what a gem this land was, and buy it up. She couldn't bear to imagine the day when the notice would be removed from the tree and she'd see the gate freshly painted, and possibly even spot the new owner, driving in and out, tending to the garden, sitting on the balcony and looking out over the endless view.

"Erba, you're tormenting me," she chastised the goat.

Olivia remembered that Charlotte had said she'd bring some food for the cat. She couldn't resist pushing open the squeaky gate and walking up to the porch to see if it had been eaten.

Charlotte had placed two bowls in the shady corner of the porch. One was half filled with water, and the other had been licked spotlessly clean. Olivia saw a distinctive paw print in the dust nearby.

Then she heard a mew, coming from the shadows at the far end of the porch.

"Kitty!" Encouraged, Olivia got onto her hands and knees and stretched out her fingers, wiggling them enticingly. "Here, kitty. Did you enjoy the food?"

The cat still looked wary, but not as fearful as it had the first time she'd seen it. It watched her for a moment before washing its paw.

"Well, you seem calmer already," Olivia told the cat, who glanced back up at her. "I'll bring you more food tomorrow. You'll be tame in no time. Beautiful cat."

As she climbed to her feet, Olivia felt a pang of regret, because at the end of the summer, she and Charlotte would be heading back home, and the cat would remain here, having to endure winter with nobody to feed or care for it anymore.

"We can tame you by then, I'm sure," Olivia promised the cat. "I'll try and find you a home before I leave, I promise."

Then her phone rang.

Startled by the noise, the cat darted away and disappeared.

"Damn," said Olivia, rummaging in her purse. She looked down at the incoming number and nearly dropped her phone.

"What?" she said aloud, in a high, shrill voice.

Matt was calling.

What on earth was going on?

Olivia stared at the incoming number, flabbergasted. Should she even answer? Perhaps this was a misdial, and he'd meant to phone someone else, and when she did answer he would scream at her for taking the call and then hang up.

It could also be that he'd found another of her personal items in one of his carry-ons and had thought of a few more names to call her.

She was going to leave it but then, almost on autopilot, she found herself pressing the green button.

"Hello?" she said guardedly.

"Olivia! I'm so glad you answered."

Clearly he'd meant to phone her, and even more weirdly, he sounded pleased to be talking to her.

Looking out across the hills, at the last bright traces of the setting sun, Olivia felt a sense of unreality. Here she was, speaking to someone on the other side of the world whom she'd thought she would never hear from again.

"How are you?" she asked, realizing how idiotic the words sounded after everything that had happened between them, but unable to think of what else to say.

Ignoring any further pleasantries, Matt got straight to the point.

"Your mother told me you went to Italy for the summer."

Olivia's eyes narrowed. What had her mother been up to?

"Did she call you?" Olivia asked, trying to get a better picture of what had happened.

"She messaged me and I called her."

"Ah," Olivia said.

"I was going to call you anyway."

Olivia frowned. What was going on? Matt's tone sounded humble and apologetic and his words were likewise.

Well, here she was, standing under an olive tree. It was timely that he was offering her an olive branch. Perhaps he didn't want to leave their argument unresolved and she had to acknowledge that was mature and sensible of him.

Matt's next words almost knocked her off her feet.

"I made a terrible mistake. I acted rashly and thoughtlessly. Liv, I should never have broken up with you. It was idiotic of me. I've been missing you ever since."

Olivia opened and closed her mouth, feeling like a fish out of water. Erba glanced at her with mild interest.

"You're on vacation in Bermuda with your new girlfriend," she spluttered out eventually. "What are you doing calling me about this?"

"The conference lasted three days. I didn't stay on afterwards. I came home." He cleared his throat, sounding embarrassed. "Um, Leigh is no longer with the company. She has accepted a personal assistant job in London and is moving there as we speak."

So something had gone wrong between him and his new girlfriend? Olivia wondered what had happened.

"I was such an idiot, Liv. I can't believe I threw away everything I had with you. I want to ask you if you would make a fresh start. Please come home. I'm missing you. I want to take a vacation with you. I would like us to relook at our lives, as a couple. We need to go forward in a new way, together."

As he spoke, Olivia found all the memories rushing back.

The fancy restaurant meals they had shared, the red roses he bought her every Valentine's Day and the white roses he bought her every birthday. How proud she'd felt when she'd gone on an outing or a date with him, and how generously he'd contributed toward the apartment's costs as well as their general expenses.

Matt hadn't been the perfect boyfriend by any means, but he had been good to her.

Her mother's words came back to her and now Olivia found herself considering them seriously. Matt was wealthy, and he would provide her with much-needed security, especially now, when getting another job might prove difficult.

Olivia paced along the sandy drive, turning away from the gate and heading up the hillside. She weaved her way through the shrubs and tussocks of grass, thinking about the implication of his words and also about her own misguided life choices.

As a couple. That was what Matt had said.

"You're right, Matt," she found herself saying softly. "I've missed you, too."

All she'd done in Italy was get herself into trouble. It had been a crazy interlude in her life, a wild adventure, but this wasn't ever going to be her reality. How could it be? How could she have had the audacity to think this place was where she belonged? It was a foreign country, with different customs, where she didn't even understand much of the language.

Matt's words brought home to her that she was living in a fantasy world, one that could never be real.

"I know you're probably angry at me. We can sit down and discuss it," Matt added. "There's been fault on both sides, so we need to look at a way forward that will work for both of us."

"Hold on a minute."

Olivia paused, picking a bright, fragrant flower from a bush.

Had he just said "fault on both sides"?

She'd thought everything was OK, in fact great, between them until the moment he'd broken up with her and admitted to cheating.

How could there be fault on both sides if he'd never told her that anything she did was wrong?

Common sense prevailed. Of course, that was what they would need to discuss. Probably, she was far too sensitive, and that in itself was a problem. Dealing with matters in an adult way meant talking through these issues.

"What is it?" Matt sounded anxious.

"Nothing," Olivia said. "Nothing. Please go on."

"Like I said, a vacation together will be a must. I'm very busy at work during August and our team has to go away on a company cruise for a week, but I was thinking you and I could do a long weekend in late July."

So the vacation had already been downgraded to nothing more than a quick mini-break?

Olivia was about to argue that they needed at least a week away, and she wasn't prepared to compromise on that, when she saw it.

Directly in front of her, shooting up from the stony ground, tall and strong, with a thick stem and beautiful wide, green leaves.

Olivia stared in astonishment at the bunches of white grapes. This wild vine was festooned with them, it was bearing prolifically.

Rare, white grapes grew naturally in this stony ground. This property could become a vineyard. It could, and it was showing her so, right now, at this exact moment.

Was she going to sell herself short, go home, and get back together with a man who'd cheated on her once and would inevitably do so again?

Or was she going to follow her dreams, however mad and unattainable they might be, because that was part of the adventure of life?

In that moment, staring at the wild vine, Olivia made her choice.

"I'm sorry, Matt," she said. "Thank you for calling, but no. I've decided to stay in Italy. Goodbye."

She heard him start to speak—spluttering out rapid and astounded words, but she didn't listen to them.

She disconnected and for good measure, turned her phone off, so she couldn't be tempted to take another call from him. Although she didn't think he would call now. She'd made her position clear. There was no going back—not now, not anymore.

"I've done it," she said aloud, her voice high and shocked. "I've really done it now. I've made my decision. I've said no to Matt and yes to Italy. I think I just accepted a marriage proposal from Tuscany. I'm wedded to the land now, just like Marcello." She let out a burst of incredulous laughter. "This is my life, here. I have to make it work now. Somehow, I have to."

Without any clue as to how she might achieve this, Olivia headed down the hill.

She felt triumphant, as if she'd defeated a demon that she hadn't even known about. A surprise, pop-up demon that had almost hijacked her life and forced her back onto a path she would have regretted.

She couldn't wait to tell Charlotte about her decision.

In another fifteen minutes, Olivia was home, marching eagerly up the paved drive with Erba trotting behind.

Quickly, she opened the front door.

"You won't believe what just happened, Charlotte," she called, stepping inside and closing the door behind her so that Erba couldn't follow into the lounge. "I just got called by Matt. My ex. And I told him—"

As she turned, Olivia's words cut off and she blinked in astonishment.

Sitting on the couch next to Charlotte, with a glass of wine in front of him, was a man whose handsome features Olivia recognized from at least a hundred Instagram photos. This was Patrick, Charlotte's ex—the man she had been going to marry, but had called it off and gone to Italy to regroup.

Now, here he was, staring at Olivia in alarm, as if her arrival had come as a nasty shock.

Chapter Twenty Seven

"Hello. You must be Patrick," Olivia said, breaking the tense silence. Patrick smiled, although the expression looked forced. He stood up and held out his hand.

"Hi. And you are?"

"This is Olivia," Charlotte said hastily. Turning to him, she said, "I hadn't got around to telling you yet. She's staying in the other bedroom." Then she turned to Olivia. "Patrick arrived this evening. He called me when the plane landed, and I went to fetch him from the airport. We've just got back."

Olivia stared at Charlotte in amazement. Charlotte couldn't have known he was coming to Italy or she would have told Olivia. So this had been a complete surprise. No wonder Charlotte had left La Leggenda in such a hurry, and abandoned her questioning of Olivia's prime suspect.

How did Charlotte feel about the bombshell of his arrival?

Olivia looked closely at her friend.

Charlotte looked happy, as if she was pleased Patrick was here. She was smiling, as if she was relieved that everything was back to normal and as if breaking off the engagement and flying to Italy had been a mere blip on the radar.

Patrick placed his hand protectively on Charlotte's knee.

"Nice to see you," Olivia said. She felt wary of his presence, after what Charlotte had shared with her about him being a sponger. Yes, he was tall and good-looking, but what if that was the start and end of his positive qualities?

"Patrick flew to Italy to surprise me," Charlotte said. "His dad bought the ticket yesterday."

"You're not the only one who's surprised," Olivia said. Her head was still whirling at the weird coincidence of both their exes making contact on the same day.

"Have you ladies had dinner yet?" Patrick asked. "I didn't eat on the plane. I get airsick if I do."

"You haven't eaten on the whole flight?" Charlotte asked, sounding concerned. "Why don't we head to the restaurant down the road? Would you like a pizza?"

"Pizza sounds good, babes."

Frowning in bemusement, Olivia followed them down the road.

She was struggling to understand why Charlotte had taken Patrick back so readily. There had been valid reasons for calling off the wedding. She'd told Olivia all about them. The main one was that Charlotte felt she was being used. That Patrick was relying on her to support him and that the relationship was unequal.

Olivia decided she would use her newly acquired investigative skills to assess whether the situation had changed.

She had already identified the first red flag, which Charlotte hadn't even appeared to notice. Patrick hadn't even paid for his own ticket. His father had. So clearly he didn't have a job, and was still relying on other people to pay his way.

If Charlotte was happy, though, did it matter?

The question was—how happy was she? If she'd been so ecstatic about this behavior why had she called off the wedding?

Olivia tuned into their conversation.

"How is your job search going?" Charlotte asked him.

"Oh, I got a job. I got a job, babes," Patrick explained airily.

"Really?"

Olivia could hear a world of admiration and relief in Charlotte's voice.

"Yeah. It was an interesting two weeks. Then I came here."

"They let you take leave? Or are you working remotely?" Now Olivia picked up some doubt.

"The job ended. I was helping my cousin design his new company workspace. We were sending ideas for the layout back and forth via email. It was really cool."

Red flag, Olivia decided. This was unacceptable. It had sounded promising until he'd homed in on the details, whereupon all his credentials had collapsed. This didn't sound like a real job. It was just doing a relative a favor.

Frustrated, she wondered how Charlotte could be accepting this. Wasn't she starting to see a few flags herself?

"And now? What are you doing now, gorgeous?" Charlotte asked.

"Oh, is this the pizza place? Quaint." Adroitly, Patrick changed the subject.

They sat down in the courtyard and looked through the simple menu. Olivia checked automatically behind her to make sure Erba hadn't followed, but there was no sign of the goat. She must have decided to turn in early at the villa.

"We usually have the margherita pizza and a glass of wine," Charlotte said.

"Sounds good, but since I'm here, we should splurge on a bottle of sparkling wine. Maybe two bottles. How about the Franciacorta, to celebrate?"

"Sure!" Charlotte smiled, her misgivings of a moment ago clearly forgotten. "What a perfect opportunity. I love sparkling wine."

"So, how long are we staying here for, babes?" Patrick asked. "You've booked this villa for the summer, right?"

"Yes, that's right."

Patrick squeezed her hand.

"I'm so glad. I've always wanted to come to Italy and just as I was in need of accommodation, you booked this villa. You're amazing, Charlotte."

Huge red flag, Olivia decided. This was so big it should actually be a red tarpaulin.

This wasn't about Charlotte, not at all. It was all about Patrick and his needs. Olivia wasn't being unfair by judging him, she was being honest.

How was she going to share her feelings with Charlotte, and help prevent her from making the same mistake again? Captivated by Patrick's show of affection, would Charlotte even listen to her, or would this end up destroying their friendship?

The pizzas arrived, interrupting her thoughts.

Olivia ate quickly, planning to leave as soon as she was finished, because she couldn't take much more of this and had no idea how she could warn her friend what a leech this man was.

It seemed that Patrick and Charlotte were also hungry, because they ate their pizzas as fast as she did. Olivia was still seated at the table when Patrick called for the bill.

At least he's paying, she thought, her annoyance tinged with relief that finally, he was doing something right.

But as the bill arrived, Patrick got up.

"Just going to the bathroom, babes," he said. "You'll sort this one out? Are we getting a cab back, or walking home?" He kissed her hair. "You decide."

Then he wound his way through the tables, heading to the restrooms.

Olivia downed her glass of sparkling wine. They'd ended up ordering two bottles of the expensive wine, and Charlotte was looking worried as she calculated the tip.

"We'll split it," she said firmly. She took out her wallet and passed over some cash.

"Oh, Olivia, are you sure?" Charlotte asked, glancing up anxiously.

"The question is, are you sure?" Olivia said.

Charlotte blinked rapidly. "What do you mean?" she asked.

Olivia had only a couple of minutes to get her point across. This was going to be an elevator pitch, and there was a real risk that it would have the wrong result, and destroy their friendship. Even so, she couldn't stay quiet on this. For Charlotte's sake, honesty had to prevail.

She gathered her thoughts, knowing that this was now or never.

"I mean you're being used. There was a reason why you called the wedding off, and he's doing it again. He's sponging off you. Ordering expensive wine and assuming someone else will pay for it is unacceptable. That job didn't sound like a real job, either."

She took another breath and continued with the second phase of her elevator pitch.

"Most of all I dislike his arrogance, assuming that you'll fit him into your life again even though he only called you when he needed a ride from the airport. Now you're going to hemorrhage money for the rest of the summer so that he can tick off everything on his bucket list. I don't think you should let him. I think—"

Olivia's elevator pitch was cut short by Patrick's return.

He squeezed Charlotte's shoulders.

"Are we ready to go, babes? Cab or walk?"

Olivia held her breath. This was the deciding moment, where Charlotte would reveal if Olivia's words had hit home, or simply caused hurt.

Her mind raced as she wondered if there were any rooms to rent in the area.

Then Charlotte spoke, smiling up at Patrick, without looking at Olivia at all.

"Let's get a cab, gorgeous," she said, and Olivia felt disappointment crush her.

She'd failed. All she'd done was to destroy her oldest friendship. It was too late to take back her words, but she bitterly regretted them.

Sitting in the front seat of the cab, because Charlotte and Patrick were occupying the back, Olivia berated herself for her reckless advice. Just because she was a superb goat trainer didn't mean she was a good relationship counselor. She'd said the wrong thing, and acted in a way that had driven Charlotte straight into Patrick's arms.

There was barely time for Olivia to have fully explored her regret over her life choices, before the cab pulled up outside the front door.

"Do you have cash on you, babes, or will this guy accept your card?" Patrick asked.

Charlotte turned to the driver.

"Would you mind waiting a minute?" she asked.

"*Si.*" He nodded.

Charlotte got out of the cab and hurried inside.

Olivia had a sick feeling in her stomach. She'd destroyed her oldest friendship and would have to leave. The least she could do was pay the driver herself. Maybe she could ask him to come back in an hour, once she'd packed her bags and figured out where to go.

Olivia rummaged in her bag, looking to see if she had enough available cash.

Patrick clearly didn't have any intention of contributing. He whistled a tune as he unbuckled his seatbelt and opened his door.

Then Olivia heard him utter a surprised, "Hey!"

Charlotte was walking out again, wheeling his suitcase behind her.

"What the hell?" Patrick squealed.

"Please would you take the signore to the airport?" Charlotte told the driver. She handed him her credit card. "You can charge the two trips together."

Then she opened the trunk and stashed his case inside.

"Wait! What's going on here? Babes, what are you doing? Is this a joke?"

Patrick sounded agonized.

"It's not a joke," Charlotte said. "I don't want you here. You arrived without asking me. You assumed I'd be fine with having you here, but I'm not. You didn't even pay for the expensive wine you ordered."

"Babes! I didn't think to do it! I was distracted by your wonderful companionship. Of course I can pay," Patrick protested, but Charlotte shook her head.

"That's not the point. The point is you were taking advantage. Just like you were hoping to get free accommodations for the summer, and have me pick up all the bills. I'm sorry, Patrick. Being cute and charming is not enough anymore. It's worn off. My best advice is to find someone more accommodating back in the States. I'm sure you won't have a problem. I'm here with my friend, who is supportive and loyal and who, incidentally, pointed out that you're behaving like a user, not a boyfriend. And I agree. Please move your leg back inside."

Charlotte stepped forward and grasped the cab's door.

Patrick didn't resist. He had a stunned look on his face, as if he couldn't believe what was happening.

"Hope you have a comfortable flight home," Charlotte said, and slammed the door.

Hastily, Olivia scrambled out of the car. She had been frozen in her seat as this drama unfolded.

"Yes, safe flight, Patrick. Enjoy!" she said in fake-cheerful tones.

They watched as the cab turned, and the taillights receded into the distance.

CHAPTER TWENTY EIGHT

When Olivia arrived at La Leggenda the following morning, her first stop was the winemaking building.

"Stay!" she told Erba as she reached the building's high, imposing doors.

Obediently, Erba jumped into a lavender pot and ripped one of the plants out by its roots.

Olivia felt a glow of pride as she rubbed the goat's forehead affectionately. She was an exceptionally intelligent goat, and attractive, too. Of course, some of the credit for Erba's compliance surely had to go to herself, as the trainer.

Olivia walked inside, taking a moment to breathe in the fragrance of slowly fermenting wine, overlaid by well-seasoned wood from the massive barrels. If she was able to keep working here, she could spend more time in this place, learning the secrets of winemaking.

"It will happen," she promised herself.

Her goal today was simple. No matter what it took, she was going to solve the mystery of Luigi's murder, and clear her name.

She walked through the tasting room in search of Nadia, noticing one of the assistants look at her in horror and duck behind a barrel. Olivia didn't care. She had her plan in place, and a winery worker publicly avoiding her was not going to derail it.

She found the vintner in the back office, busy on her computer. Nadia's dark hair was tied back and her face was intent as she tapped at the keys.

Olivia hesitated at the door as she looked up.

"Hi," she said. "I'm sorry to interrupt. Can I please ask you a question?"

She expected the same fearful reaction from Nadia as she'd had previously, but to her surprise, the vintner nodded reluctantly.

"I suppose you can," she said.

"Is it convenient? I can come back later," Olivia said.

"I am busy with routine admin. I can take a quick break. Sit down." Nadia gestured impatiently to a chair.

"I thought you might be suspicious of me," Olivia confessed, taking the seat. "Everyone else here seems to be."

Nadia shrugged.

"I will wait for the police to finish their investigation. They must decide who is guilty," she snapped.

"I want to ask you a question about the evening of Luigi's death," Olivia said, hoping that this wouldn't cause Nadia to fly into a temper.

"What?" she asked suspiciously.

"You said Marcello was going out, but he arrived at the tasting room just after we did. I was wondering if you knew where he went," Olivia said.

She held her breath as Nadia frowned.

"He had a meeting. He only told me about it in the afternoon. I am not sure where, or who it was with. Have you asked him? Why are you here, asking me?"

"I will ask him. I wanted to check with you first."

Olivia had hoped to gather the information without having to confront Marcello directly, but she saw now that it would not be possible.

"I usually do ask him, or he tells me," Nadia added thoughtfully. "But our day was so busy that this time it didn't happen."

That made Olivia even more suspicious.

"Is there anything else you want to ask? Because I have a busy morning ahead," the vintner said, in a tone that told Olivia her time was up.

"Nothing, thank you," she said humbly.

She left the winemaking premises wondering how to phrase her questions to Marcello.

He was handsome and charming, but Olivia reminded herself that so was Patrick, hopefully now Charlotte's ex for good, and that hadn't made his behavior any more acceptable.

She had seen only yesterday how charming men were able to get away with more, and as the winery owner, Marcello might have been above suspicion. She had observed how he reacted to Luigi and knew that there was no love lost between them. Also, despite the sommelier's in-depth knowledge, Marcello had surely realized his arrogance and combative attitude was causing problems with customers.

Had Marcello gotten away with murder?

It was a terrible thought, especially when she remembered how he'd squeezed her hand so intimately as they had shared a glass of the Miracolo blend. And how he'd looked into her eyes so that she felt she was drowning in his gaze.

Olivia told herself to stop it. This line of thought would get her nowhere. This was a serious matter. Marcello was a murder suspect who could well be trying to hide his guilt. Olivia resolved to keep a cool head and question him herself, as soon as she had the chance.

At lunch time, Olivia saw Marcello coming out of the restaurant, and rushed to meet him.

"Olivia. You have been doing well today, I see. The sales reflect it."

His smile was as warm as ever, but this time Olivia felt a chill of fear. What was behind it? How well did she really know him, and had he fooled her?

"It's been very busy." She took a deep breath. "Marcello, I was wondering something."

"What were you wondering?" His eyes sparkled as he regarded her, making Olivia think along completely different lines for a moment.

She dragged her attention back to the matter at hand. Proper investigators did not allow themselves to be sidetracked by charm. Or handsome features, or incredible dark blue eyes.

"On the night Luigi was killed, you went to a meeting. I remember Nadia mentioned it. But you were at the winery when his body was found. I can't help thinking about this and feeling confused. I guess I need to get the timeline right in my mind, in case the police question me about it," Olivia gabbled, aware she was turning bright red and that despite her excuse, Marcello must have a good idea of what she was asking and why.

"You are right. I was called in the afternoon and invited to a meeting at Casa D'Orio, the big winery across the valley. The owner, Enzo D'Orio, wanted to discuss producing a collaboration wine. But when I arrived, I could not find him there, so I came immediately back. As I walked in, I heard Nadia scream."

"Oh," Olivia said.

It sounded like a very flimsy story to her.

Marcello was so pleasant, such a gentleman, but she reminded herself that he was also a hot-blooded Italian and that powerful emotions could have been simmering below his compassionate façade.

Perhaps they had boiled over at the wrong time, and he had acted in the heat of the moment.

She smiled back at him.

"Meeting with the opposition? Is that not like sleeping with the enemy?"

She thought she saw Marcello's pupils dilate when she spoke the last words, and forced her knees not to buckle in response.

"You are right. It seems unusual. However, we do collaborate with a number of other wineries, and I discussed the possibility with Enzo a few years ago."

Olivia realized that the meeting itself would be easy to confirm. An opposition winemaker would not lie to protect a rival. Additionally, phone records would prove him honest, or otherwise.

She couldn't pursue this line of questioning any further, but would have to decide on her next step.

Marcello seemed about to say something else, but at that moment, Nadia hurried in.

"Detective Caputi is on her way. She asked us to make ourselves available urgently. Perhaps there has been a breakthrough in the case." She glanced at Olivia. "Perhaps they have sufficient evidence to make an arrest."

Olivia froze.

Her clumsy, amateur attempts at investigation to clear her name meant nothing now. The detective was the one who held the power and who had the final word. How had Olivia been able to ignore this truth? Of course, Detective Caputi had been working tirelessly to put together a timeframe, and circumstantial evidence, to prove Olivia had done it. It was the only easy, neat solution to this complicated problem.

Nadia looked triumphant, her expression telling Olivia she knew she had been right all along.

Gesturing in a way that she hoped would seem casual, Olivia managed to drop her purse. It landed on the floor with a thump and the contents spilled out.

"Sorry," Olivia said, kneeling down to collect the items. She felt herself turning red. There were a few embarrassing personal items visible among the spillage, and she knew Marcello was looking.

Nadia was looking, too, but not at the belongings that Olivia was hastily scooping together.

"That paper. What is that?"

Olivia looked up, cupping her hands protectively over her assembled items. "Excuse me?" she said.

"This. What is this?"

Nadia bent down and picked up a scrap of paper lying nearby.

For a moment, Olivia was confused. What was it? Had she written something down earlier and lost it in her purse? She didn't clean out her bag often enough. This could be something to do with her flight, or even a note she'd made back in Chicago.

Or it could have been dropped by a customer, and not belong to her at all.

"I've no idea—" she began, but Nadia gasped.

"Call the detective, quick! She must come quickly!"

"Why?" Olivia felt sweat spring out on her palms. What had happened?

"This is the code for the safe." She glared down at Olivia. "The safe in my office, where you met me this morning. The secret safe, where the most important wine recipe we own is stored—the formula for Miracolo. You were the one that killed Luigi! You were planning to steal it. Luigi must have found out what you were going to do, so you killed him!"

Nadia glared accusingly at Olivia. Marcello was staring at her with horror in his eyes.

"Police!" Nadia shouted to a passing assistant. "Call them! Now!"

CHAPTER TWENTY NINE

"Wait!" Olivia whispered.

She tried to suppress her rising panic, knowing she had to think calmly to save herself now. Was this a setup? Had Nadia planted the code on her? How could Olivia explain that she had no idea where it had come from or what it was?

Olivia's heart missed a beat as she remembered.

This was the scrap of paper she'd picked up from Luigi's office during her investigation yesterday. She'd kept it just in case.

Olivia had been disappointed after her search, thinking no hard evidence had come to light. Well, she had been wrong. She'd found the crucial piece of evidence, but now it was being used against her.

"I didn't do it," she insisted.

Nadia placed her hands on her hips and stared her down. "Oh, yes, you did. Don't try and lie your way out of this."

"I found the paper in Luigi's office."

"You are making that up."

Olivia glanced at Marcello pleadingly. There seemed to be no way to prove her innocence now. Would he intervene?

To her dismay, she saw a resigned sadness in his eyes.

"I think you must go to my office and wait for the police there," he told her softly. "We will have to allow them to manage the situation for now."

Olivia swallowed hard. At this critical time, Marcello was remaining neutral. Well, she guessed he had no alternative, faced with compelling evidence to the contrary.

She trudged down the corridor to his office. This was where she would have to wait for the hammer blow to fall. She'd done nothing. This was all so unfair, but there didn't seem to be a way out. Who would believe her version was true?

There was another solution, Olivia suddenly realized.

At the end of the corridor was an exit door that led out to the back courtyard.

She could slip through it and escape. The courtyard opened onto a garden, and beyond that was a track that led to the service driveway. She could take that road and be back at the villa before the police arrived. If she called a cab to the airport, she could be on a plane before they realized what she'd done.

She could take the first available plane. She didn't mind at all where it would go. Anywhere would do.

Emboldened by her decision, Olivia quickened her pace. She hurried past Marcello's office and opened the back door. The hinges squeaked, and she jumped, glancing round to make sure Marcello hadn't heard. He was still in the tasting room. Perhaps a guest had arrived. That would be a stroke of luck for her, and it was about time she got lucky.

Olivia sneaked through the door and closed it behind her.

The fresh outside air tasted of freedom.

Faintly, around the corner, she could hear the hum of voices and clink of cutlery from the restaurant. Olivia turned the other way, heading through the archway into the garden.

Beyond it was the path that would take her to the gate.

Determinedly, Olivia strode down the service driveway. She hoped that Erba would not notice she was leaving, because if she followed Olivia, it would draw attention to her.

Given the unusual time of day, she hoped Erba would be busy elsewhere.

The warm breeze tugged at her hair, blowing it across her face as she turned to check behind her. Nobody there. So far, her getaway was proceeding without a hitch, but Olivia's hands felt damp and her heart was lodged in her throat. She knew she wouldn't be able to relax until she was actually on a plane out of here. Never mind that—she'd only feel safe when the plane had taken off.

Then Olivia drew in a sharp breath as she saw an approaching car, the sun glinting off its roof.

She needed to hide. The closest cover was a cluster of bushes to the right.

Should she wait there while the car passed? Or should she walk confidently on, as if she had every right to be leaving the vineyard at this time?

Perhaps hiding wouldn't be necessary. Time was of the essence, and the driver was probably bringing in a delivery.

As the car drew closer, Olivia began to change her mind.

This car looked familiar. It was a gray Fiat. The police had arrived in gray Fiats on the evening of Luigi's murder.

"Uh-oh," Olivia whispered.

It seemed as if Detective Caputi had decided to use the service road.

"Well, this doesn't look incriminating at all," Olivia muttered, preparing to sprint for the bushes.

Then she whirled around as, from behind her, she heard a delighted bleat. Erba had seen her and was capering down the road toward her.

There was no escape now. Olivia had effectively been blocked.

The car slowed down as it reached her and the detective buzzed the window down. She looked grim, as did the uniformed police officer in the passenger seat. Clearly, they had been apprised of the situation.

"Were you going for a walk?" Detective Caputi asked. Sarcasm dripped from the words.

"I was just—" Olivia tried, smiling weakly.

The police officer leaned over and the back door swung open.

"Get in," Caputi snapped.

Olivia perched on a chair in Marcello's office, seated between Detective Caputi and the uniformed police officer. Staring from one to the other in consternation, she knew was no way she could try and escape again. They would grab her before she even got to her feet.

Olivia suddenly realized that life was trying to teach her a lesson here, which she was stubbornly refusing to learn.

What had she done under pressure?

She'd tried to run away.

It was the police investigation equivalent of quitting her job on the spot, and Olivia felt frustrated by her inability to break free of this distressing character trait.

This was the third time now!

Probably, the best time to have a deep personal insight was not while she was surrounded by detectives and under incipient arrest, but even so Olivia resolved that this time she would not shy away from uncomfortable truths.

She had to change her ways! Life was showing her clearly, and in a forceful manner, that running away would not work out for her.

In that case, instead of panicking, she needed to remain mentally calm and agile. She had to reason her way out of this predicament like a grown-up, rather than attempting to flee.

There must be some means she could use to convince this stern detective of her innocence. Were all her newly acquired investigative skills going to go to waste? Or could she somehow find a way to prove that she was right and they were wrong?

"I was coming out to re-interview some of the winery staff, who all seemed to think the same person was guilty of the murder," Caputi said to Marcello and Nadia, who were seated opposite, listening solemnly. She gave Olivia a sidelong glance, and Olivia felt herself wilt. "However, it seems we may have made a major breakthrough."

Olivia glanced at her nervously. She still had no idea how she was going to clear her name, and now the detective was setting up her tape recorder.

"I would like you to give me an exact account of what happened earlier," she said to Nadia and Marcello. "Please be as detailed as possible, as this will form part of the evidence if she is found guilty."

Olivia began to hyperventilate. She didn't want to spend time in jail, and Charlotte and Erba would be lonely without her. She guessed the bail would be set very high—too high for her to afford at this point, and there was nobody else she could ask.

She needed to come up with a compelling argument at lightning speed if she was going to avoid being arrested, even temporarily.

As she gulped in air, she picked up the scent of fresh-baked bread wafting through from the restaurant. It was shocking to think that if she was arrested, she would no longer be able to taste this luxury, nor be allowed to enjoy the simple freedom of walking to a bakery to buy a warm, crispy loaf.

Perhaps it was the extra oxygen from her rapid breathing, or perhaps it was the aroma of bread that made her think back to the drive they had taken on her first day in Italy. Either way, puzzle pieces suddenly slotted into place in Olivia's mind. She had an idea.

In fact, as her thoughts solidified, she realized it was more than an idea, it was a certainty.

Her theory covered everything that had occurred since she'd been working at the winery, and it made complete sense. She had solved the mystery.

The only problem was that it might be too late.

"Wait!" she shouted, as Detective Caputi's finger hovered over the Record button.

Nadia jumped visibly, clearly on the edge of her nerves. Marcello looked up at her and Olivia saw hope in his eyes.

The detective turned to her, frowning.

"What?" she snapped.

Olivia collected her thoughts. Never mind an elevator pitch, she had to give a skyrocket pitch now. She guessed she had roughly five seconds before the detective's patience ran out and she pushed ahead regardless.

"I need you to check something before we go any further. Please. It's critically important."

"You are wasting police time," Nadia hissed.

Detective Caputi compressed her lips and stared piercingly at Olivia.

"What do you want us to check?" she asked.

Olivia took a deep breath.

"I want you to look inside the safe in Nadia's office."

"Really?" the vintner jeered. "Would you like to see what else is in there, that you can plan to steal as well?" She turned to the detective. "This is ridiculous. You are correct, this woman is wasting police time. Also, her behavior is stressing me out. She is trying to find another chance to run away. I have a wine to blend today, still, and I need a calm mind. Can you please arrest her now?"

Detective Caputi nodded.

"I agree. This question is frivolous. You are obstructing the course of justice, and looking for another opportunity to escape." She leaned forward to the tape recorder and Olivia looked down in despair. She felt as if her world was crumbling around her.

They hadn't listened. They wouldn't do what she was asking. Her theory might never see the light of day—and nor might she, if this scary detective managed to gather enough evidence.

Then Marcello said, "Wait!"

Olivia's head jerked up.

He wasn't looking at her, but instead was staring at the police detective with the expression she'd seen him use a few times in the past. With the softened eyes, the tilt of his head that sent his dark hair falling over his forehead, and the hint of a smile, this was Marcello at his most charming.

Perhaps he'd taken sides at last, and was fighting for her.

"I think, before you say yes or no, you should ask Olivia why she wants to do this. Does that not seem reasonable?" His eyes met hers for just a moment and she saw unexpected warmth in them. More than that, she sensed his belief in her.

"Why?" the detective asked, turning to her. There was no mercy in her gaze at all. Her expression told Olivia that whatever she said had better be good.

"To see if the recipe is still there," Olivia said.

"Of course it will be there," Nadia cried in frustration. "You have been walking around with the safe code in your purse, waiting for a chance to steal it."

"Exactly," Olivia said. "I was walking around here. Doing my job. Running the tasting room. So if the recipe is still there, then yes, you can say I am guilty of the murder and I was waiting for a chance to access the safe. But if the recipe is not there, then I would already have stolen it. So why would I still be working here? I would have left immediately."

There was a thoughtful silence in the room and she saw Marcello nod approvingly.

"All right," Detective Caputi said. "Let us go and view the safe."

They stood up. Olivia noticed how the two police officers kept her carefully bracketed between them. There was no way she was going to be able to make a run for it.

She felt sick with anticipation. She was sure her theory was correct, but what if it wasn't?

"Everyone, out," Nadia called as she marched into the winemaking hall, leading the way, with Marcello close behind. "Please leave the premises. The police are busy here now."

She gave a dramatic sweep of her arm, and the workers hurried to the door.

There was barely room for all of them in Nadia's small office. Olivia was shunted into place on the opposite side of the desk, with the uniformed policeman between her and the door.

She felt breathless with anxiety. She knew she was right—this was the only solution—but all the same, what if she was wrong? She would have made everything far worse with this last-ditch attempt at saving herself.

Nadia headed straight to the safe. Marcello stood close behind her, blocking the others' view as she turned the dial carefully.

Olivia heard the scrape of heavy metal hinges as the door opened.

Then Nadia's voice, loud and full of triumph, announcing the worst possible news, the outcome Olivia had thought to be impossible.

"The recipe is still here! She was lying!"

Chapter Thirty

Olivia let out a horrified squeak. She'd been certain her theory was watertight. She'd reasoned logically, and it was the only explanation that made sense. What had just happened was impossible, a disaster. How could the recipe still be in the safe?

She could see that Detective Caputi's patience, never plentiful, had evaporated entirely.

"Let us return and continue the interview," she snapped. Glaring at Olivia, she said, "This will count against you."

Olivia's eyes stung with tears. This was unjust, humiliating, and downright impossible.

She stumbled as she turned to leave, and the police officer grasped her arm. Not to help her stay on her feet, she was sure, but to keep her from making a final, desperate run for it.

Then, from behind her, Marcello spoke, sounding confused.

"This is not the recipe, Nadia."

There was a short, intense silence. Olivia looked around in amazement. She could feel her heart thudding.

"Yes it is," the vintner insisted. "There's only one document in this safe, and that is it."

"But it isn't. Look." Marcello sounded alarmed as he drew a slim plastic folder out of the safe. "This is where it was kept, but someone has substituted the pages. Instead of the printed formula for the wine, I see there is now a recipe for pasta carbonara."

"What? You are joking." Nadia's voice was high.

"'Step One: Put a large pot of water on to boil,'" Marcello read. "'Step Two: Finely chop 100 grams of pancetta, removing any rind beforehand. Step Three: Beat three large eggs in a medium bowl, seasoning them with—'"

"All right, all right." Nadia grabbed the folder from him. "There is no need to go through the entire recipe. We all know how to make pasta carbonara. What I want to know is why this is now here, and where is my wine formula?"

Looking panicked, she flicked through the folder. It didn't take long, because there were only two pages.

"'Step Twelve. Serve immediately, sprinkling on the remaining cheese and adding black pepper to taste,'" Marcello read over her shoulder as Nadia gaped at the second page in disbelief.

"You are right." Nadia stared challengingly at Olivia. "The formula for the wine has disappeared. If you are so clever as to know it was not here, can you tell us where it has gone? Have you hidden it somewhere?"

"I can tell you my theory," Olivia said, pleased that her voice sounded calm, although she was shaking all over. "Marcello, you will need to make an urgent phone call. We should return to your office now. While we wait, I will explain what I think happened, and where the recipe can probably be found."

⚜ ⚜ ⚜

Half an hour later, Olivia was seated in Marcello's office. He was sitting next to her, so close that their shoulders brushed. Nadia was perched on a chair on his other side, twining her fingers together anxiously.

The atmosphere was one of tense expectation. They were waiting for the suspect to arrive, and for the conclusion to play out.

"Is there a secret to making pasta carbonara? Any insider hints? I'd love to try it sometime," Olivia said. Her mouth felt dry, but the silence was becoming uncomfortable. She needed to make some small talk.

"Thorough stirring when you add the egg mixture in is critical," Marcello told her. There was an edge to his voice that told her he was nervous, too. "Exposed to heat, the eggs can otherwise scramble, which spoils the consistency."

"You sound like you've made it often," Olivia said.

Marcello nodded. "As a single man, working hard, I have to eat well, and it is food I love. But, ideally, it is a dish for sharing."

Olivia glanced at him.

Was he flirting with her? The room felt suddenly warmer.

How should she reply? Would flirting back be taking this too far?

Then, heavy footsteps sounded outside the door and she felt Marcello tense.

There was no more time for flirting, or discussing cookery, because the guest they were waiting for had arrived.

A stocky, bearded man walked in. He was carrying a slim briefcase, and a smart, black jacket was slung over his shoulders.

"Enzo." Marcello stood up. "Thank you for joining us. I am glad we could reschedule our meeting after Luigi's tragic death. This is Olivia, our new sommelier."

"My condolences to you, Marcello and Nadia," Enzo said. He nodded at Olivia while Marcello opened a bottle of red wine.

"This is our Cabernet Sauvignon from last year. Still young, but we are pleased by how roundly it is maturing," Marcello said, as he poured four glasses. "Olivia was about to tell me an interesting story. I am sure you will not mind if she relates it to you also, over a glass of wine?"

The frown lines on Enzo's forehead deepened, but he said, "Continue."

Speaking in a voice that sounded high and squeaky, despite her best efforts, Olivia began.

"I was sitting in this office earlier on, and the window was open. I could smell the baking bread from the restaurant."

Nadia nodded. "I, too, picked up that aroma," she said.

"It made me think back to my first day in Italy, when my friend and I were driving through Collina. We saw two bakeries opposite each other in the town, and we laughed at how the owner of one was walking across the road after closing time, to photograph the other bakery's specials. It made me think about rivalry, and what lengths competitors might go to in order to gain an edge over their opponents."

"Go on?" Marcello encouraged her.

Olivia noticed that Enzo's frown had deepened into a glower. She didn't know if it was because of what she was saying, or because the La Leggenda Cabernet Sauvignon tasted better than he'd hoped it would.

Her palms felt damp as she resumed her story.

"Working closely with Luigi, I was shocked and confused by who could have killed him and why. When I thought about this, it provided me with a clue."

"What do you believe happened?" Marcello asked her.

There was a tense silence in the room.

"I know that only the Vescovi family has the safe code," Olivia said. "A week or two ago, Luigi must have watched one of you open the safe. He would have to have been in the office at the right time, and watched it happen."

Nadia cleared her throat. "The Thursday before last, I opened the safe and turned around to find Luigi standing right behind me. He immediately began shouting at me, accusing my assistant winemaker of having delivered the wrong vintage to the tasting room. It caused a huge fight, and by the time it was over, I had forgotten he might have seen the code," she said.

"A deliberate distraction," Marcello agreed thoughtfully.

Olivia nodded. "In any case, Luigi saw what the safe code was. As the head sommelier, nobody would question his authority, and he had access to the wine-making building. On the afternoon before he was killed, you and Nadia were out of the winery, taking visitors on a vineyard tour. Knowing there was nobody around, Luigi went in and stole the recipe for the Miracolo, substituting other pages in the folder so that the theft would be less obvious."

Enzo began spluttering and his face turned a deep crimson.

Olivia didn't know if it was in anger, or if he'd choked on a mouthful of the Cabernet Sauvignon. Either way, she was glad to have the solid oak desk between them, and Marcello close beside her, as she continued.

"Miracolo is the wine that every other vintner longs to be able to produce. Luigi said many times, to me, and to customers, how sought-after this wine was. I know the Vescovi family has turned down numerous offers to buy the formula. Luigi decided to betray the winery and sell it. But something went wrong when the buyer arrived."

The silence in the room was so profound that Olivia could hear the faraway clinking of cutlery in the restaurant. It was weird to think that back in the winery, business was going on as usual, with the visitors and tourists having no idea of the tense scene playing out in this small office.

"What, in your opinion, happened?" Marcello asked.

"Perhaps Luigi changed his mind, or asked for more money. At any rate, the deal was jeopardized. So the buyer grabbed the closest weapon, which ironically happened to be the last bottle of 2012 Miracolo. He hit Luigi over the head, grabbed the recipe, and ran."

"Who was the buyer?" Marcello asked.

"It was the person who arranged a meeting with you, to make sure you would be off the premises while the deal was done. The buyer of the recipe, and Luigi's killer, is Enzo D'Orio."

Olivia raised her head and looked directly into Enzo's furious eyes.

CHAPTER THIRTY ONE

Enzo's roar of rage filled the room. The wine glass shattered on the ground as he leaped to his feet, his chair banging down behind him.

"Who is this mad Americano woman and why are you listening to her? This is utterly preposterous! It is a stealthy attempt by La Leggenda to blacken my name. I will not listen to any more of this unfounded rubbish, and will instead be calling my lawyer. You will be sued for this, Marcello." He pointed a stubby finger at Olivia. "And I will sue you in my personal capacity for these slanderous lies."

He stormed toward the door, but as he opened it, he stopped in his tracks.

Detective Caputi stood in the passageway, with the uniformed policeman behind her.

"Not so fast," she said quietly, but there was steel to her tone.

Enzo stared at her, then glanced back at Marcello, and Olivia saw the first hint of fear in his eyes.

"Why not?" Enzo asked the detective. Olivia could hear the unsteadiness in his voice. He was shaken now, and dreading the worst.

"While you have been sitting here, two of my detectives have raided your winery and searched your office. Since there was probable cause, no warrant was required, and we were able to act with great speed. I have just received confirmation that they found the Miracolo recipe in the top drawer of your desk."

"What?" Enzo cried, his voice high with strain. "Impossible!"

"Apparently it has a large stain of red wine on it, but is otherwise in good condition. So, Signore Enzo D'Orio, you are formally under arrest. Anything you say may be used as evidence in a court of law. You will now accompany us to the police station."

Snorting with rage, Enzo was handcuffed in a moment, and the two police officers shepherded him out of the room. As he reached the door, he turned back to snarl at Olivia.

"You will regret this, I promise you."

Nadia leaped to her feet.

"No, she will not. She has saved us! She is part of our family now. You are the one who will regret the empty threats you are making. Get out of here, you ugly pig! I have never liked you, or your wines. The Cabernet is revolting and your Merlot tastes sour. You allow immature grapes to be used instead of having patience. You should go for a swim in a vat of Valley Wine, together with all the rats, that is where you belong. No wonder you need to steal recipes, in order to call yourself a winemaker!"

Nadia continued shouting until Enzo was well out of earshot.

Olivia let out a deep breath, feeling dizzy with relief.

She'd cracked the case and discovered who the killer was. More than that, she had been accepted by the Vescovis, and welcomed into the close-knit community at La Leggenda.

An hour later, Olivia was sitting at a table in the tasting room. Marcello was on one side of her. Antonio, still wearing his dusty jacket, had taken a break from tending the vines and was sitting opposite.

"Should we?" Marcello asked Nadia.

She thought for a while, and then nodded. "I think so. Now is a good time."

Marcello got up and took four champagne flutes from the back of the glass cupboard.

"We have been looking at introducing a sparkling wine to our portfolio," Marcello told her. "Nadia has been working on it for two years already, and we believe the time is right to taste the prototype. We were waiting for an occasion to celebrate."

Nadia hurried out of the room. A minute later, she was back, carrying a dark glass bottle, its top wrapped with gold foil.

"We will not get a better time than this. Imagine if the formula for our precious blend had been stolen. It could have happened so easily. Olivia, you have saved us. I am sorry I was such a bitch to you. I am a bitch to everyone. I even fight with my brothers most of the time. That is why I work in the winemaking building and seldom go outside."

Marcello laughed.

"Go on," he encouraged his sister. "Open it. Let us see what you have created while staying indoors and keeping your fiery temper to yourself."

Nadia passed the bottle to Antonio.

"You grew the grapes. You open it."

Carefully, Antonio peeled away the foil and untwisted the wire. The cork shot out of the bottle, followed by a head of foam.

Quickly, Antonio filled the glasses.

"To Olivia," he said.

"To Olivia," the others echoed, and they clinked their glasses together.

Blushing, feeling self-conscious about all the compliments, Olivia raised her glass. The sparkling wine had a sumptuous, toasty aroma and the bubbles tickled her nose. Enraptured, she sipped.

"It's wonderful," she gasped. "This is a masterpiece. I can't believe it's your trial version. This should go into the tasting room tomorrow."

Now it was Nadia's turn to blush, laughing.

"It still needs work. But I am pleased with it. The grapes were perfect. All I had to do was apply the correct techniques for the double fermentation, to produce the bubbles."

"Olivia, we spoke together after the police left," Marcello said, his face serious. "We would like to offer you the permanent position of head sommelier at La Leggenda. There can be no better person to look after our guests, and our tasting room."

Olivia stared at him in shock. A permanent position? This was the foothold in the winemaking industry she needed.

Her instinct was to accept it immediately, but the situation was more complicated than that. It was a life-changing offer, and that meant she would have to change her life. Was she ready to abandon everything she had back in Chicago, including the safety net of the advertising agency world? Was she prepared to take a giant leap of faith and make a brand new start here?

"It sounds amazing," she began, but Marcello held up his hand.

"Please, think it over carefully. This is a commitment, and we want you to make it after proper thought. We will put together a salary package for you, and a formal job offer, and email it through this afternoon. You can give us your answer any time, as soon as you have made up your mind."

"I'll do that," Olivia said gratefully.

Back at the villa, she opened her laptop, waiting for the ping that would mean the email had arrived. While she waited, she researched accommodations in the area, and priced cars for sale. She jotted down numbers and added them up. Would she be able to save enough to move into her own place by the end of September? A lot depended on what La Leggenda offered her, but no matter how generous the salary, Olivia was so broke that she could see it was going to be a tight squeeze.

Her email pinged, and Olivia grabbed her computer. Here it was. What did it say?

To her disappointment, she saw that the incoming mail was not from La Leggenda. It was from a man whose name sounded vaguely familiar, although she couldn't place it.

The sender was Des Whiteley, and the mail was titled, "Decision Needed."

Olivia thought that was ironic. There was only one decision she needed to make now, and this mail had no bearing on it. The sender's name sounded familiar, though, and after a moment, she realized who it was.

Des Whiteley was the CEO of Kansas Foods, the holding company of Valley Wines.

Why was he emailing her? Perhaps he wanted her input on whether or not to start his revolting wine up again under a new name. If so, she was going to give him a piece of her mind.

Mentally preparing for battle, Olivia opened it.

She read the first paragraph and then shouted, "What?"

Blinking in disbelief, she read through Des Whiteley's entire mail, and then reread it just in case she was hallucinating.

Dear Olivia,

I understand you are no longer employed by James Clark. We are seeking your advice, as we have been unhappy with the performance of JCreative after you left. It is my personal opinion that you were the only competent account manager there who gave us the results we are seeking.

Can you give me your honest opinion on whether we should keep our account with JCreative, or move it elsewhere? If we should move it, can you recommend alternative agencies that might be able to do a better job, as this is a big financial commitment for us and we are results-driven.

Finally, are you still involved in the industry at all? Would you be able to handle our account, even on a freelance basis? Without a doubt, you yourself would be our first choice.

I appreciate your honest feedback on the options we have, and please let me know if you are available.

Olivia cupped her face in her hands, mostly to keep her mouth closed, as it kept falling open.

"Well!" she said. "Seriously?"

She reread it a third time. Then she started to smile. She knew what she had to do now.

Olivia pressed Forward, and sent the mail to James. She didn't think there was a need for any covering message. Then she walked out into the garden and headed up the hillside to visit the wild vines.

When she came back ten minutes later, there were ten missed calls on her phone and it was ringing again.

CHAPTER THIRTY TWO

Olivia decided James had suffered enough. It was time to put him out of his misery by answering his eleventh phone call.

"Olivia. Olivia." James sounded more stressed than she'd ever known him to be, but at the same time his voice was quivering with false heartiness. "How wonderful to speak to you."

"I don't know if you have had time to read the mail I forwarded?" she asked, concealing a smile. She was pleased to realize her voice sounded normal. She wasn't putting on the brisk, professional persona for James any longer. She was a new and stronger person now, without that anxious need.

"Yes, yes. That mail. Yes, indeed, that mail. I did in fact read it and it's the reason why I am calling you urgently." Now James was the one who sounded anxious. "Olivia, I would like to plead with you, not just as a respected and admired colleague, but as my personal friend—I feel that after more than a decade of working together, we have become friends?"

Olivia listened to the expectant silence, and when she said nothing, James continued, his voice another octave shriller.

"As a highly esteemed colleague, I would ask you to please look after the agency that has looked after you so well. This is our biggest client by far, and I won't lie to you, times have been challenging since the Valley Wines FDA raid. A number of clients have left us. We have been forced to regroup and consolidate, and find ways to give our existing clients a thousand percent more in terms of value."

Olivia knew only too well what that meant. Extended working hours, brutally early meetings, mails being answered late into the night, last-minute briefings with impossible creative targets. She felt sorry for Bianca.

"I see," she said.

"Will you do it? Will you be willing to put in a positive word?"

Olivia took a deep breath.

"I can't see any reason to speak negatively of you and your company, James," she said. Then she added, "Especially since I know there was a temporary misunderstanding about my salary payment, which you will rectify immediately."

"Absolutely," James gushed. "You beat me to it. You beat me to it! I was about to say that your back pay and bonus will be wired immediately. It will reflect in your account before the end of the day."

"That's great timing. I'm planning to respond to Des Whiteley at the end of the day as well," Olivia said. "I'm sure my comments will be favorable. Have a good day, James."

She disconnected and gave a gleeful giggle.

What a magical reversal of circumstances. Now she had enough money to set herself up in Italy. She would be able to buy a car, and look at furnishing a nice apartment or a small house close to La Leggenda. Things were falling into place.

Or else—

Olivia sat bolt upright.

The property, that beautiful, wild, forgotten property.

Could she possibly afford it now?

"Charlotte, come with me! Quick!"

Grabbing her purse, Olivia headed out of the house at a run.

A few breathless minutes later, Olivia staggered up to the wrought iron gate, with Erba gamboling ahead and Charlotte puffing up the hill behind her.

"Power walking," her friend gasped. "That's what's been missing in my life since I've been here—not!"

"This price. What is it in dollars? Please do the math. You're the numbers person. I'm worried I'll get it wrong."

Olivia logged into her bank account. The money from James was already there.

Charlotte gave her the figure and she compared it to the total in her account.

She gave a frustrated sigh. She'd miscalculated the first time. Her guesstimation had been way off, by a large amount. She'd done the exchange rate calculation wrong. Olivia was beginning to realize that her talents did not lie in quantity conversion. She messed it up every time.

"Can you?" Charlotte asked eagerly.

Olivia shook her head. "No. I don't have enough. Not even close."

"Damn," Charlotte sympathized. "Is there any other plan you can think of? Give it some thought. I'm going to feed the cat again. I can see him waiting on the porch."

"Erba, we're not giving up yet. We need to apply our minds," Olivia told the goat, tickling the orange spot on her back. "Are you focusing? If I can think my way out of a murder charge, there must be a plan I can make to afford this place."

She followed Charlotte through the creaky gate and along the overgrown garden path.

The cat was sitting on the edge of the porch. He looked hungry, but when Charlotte came closer, he lost his nerve and darted away.

Cat food. Cats.

Olivia's thoughts were suddenly cast back to Chicago.

She'd left in such a panic that she'd all but forgotten the hurried conversation she'd had with Long-Winded Len.

He'd been wanting to buy her apartment so he could expand his cat space. How had she forgotten this? It had been a genuine offer, from a man with the means to buy, and in her panic she'd wiped it from her mind completely.

Crossing all her mental fingers, Olivia called him.

The phone rang twice, three times. Perhaps he was preoccupied with his trains.

Then he answered.

"Len, hi. It's Olivia. I'm calling you from Italy. I was wondering something. You mentioned you wanted to buy my apartment. Are you still interested?"

Half an hour later, Olivia, Charlotte, and Erba stood in a row on the porch, watching as a tiny silver Fiat drove up the winding road and into the property.

Olivia clasped her hands together tightly, hoping that there would be a positive outcome to this meeting. This was make-or-break, and she had so little room to bargain.

The car parked, and an elderly lady climbed out.

She had snow white hair and was wearing a bright purple jacket and a lime green hat.

Olivia sighed, noting the woman's silver boots. She looked like the cover model for the senior edition of *Vogue*. It was the Italian sense of style again.

She knew she could never achieve it. It was genetic, she decided. Definitely genetic.

"*Buon giorno, signorina*," the woman greeted her as Olivia hurried up, her hand outstretched. "I am Gina."

"Olivia Glass," she replied breathlessly.

"You are *Americano*?" The woman sounded surprised. "And you want to buy this old farm?"

"Yes!" Olivia exclaimed. "I came here on vacation and fell in love with it the first moment I saw it."

"You are on your own there?"

Olivia tried to force the image of Marcello's deep blue eyes out of her mind as she nodded.

"This farm has been in the family for many years," Gina explained. "And sometimes I feel, on the market for even longer. Why do you want to buy it?"

Her gaze was sharp and curious.

"I have this dream of starting up my own small winery. I've already taken a job at La Leggenda so I can learn how," Olivia gabbled.

"Wine?" Gina asked, sounding surprised.

"Yes," Olivia confessed.

"Can you pay the asking price?"

This was it. The moment of truth. Olivia's hands were shaking and her mouth felt dry.

"I was wondering if I could possibly make a lower offer," she said softly.

"For how much less?" The elderly woman's voice sounded sharp.

Olivia felt lightheaded with stress. How could she do this?

She needed a reduction of five percent. Even with the money she would receive from her apartment, she would still need a cushion to fix this place up and establish herself here. She could not afford the full asking price. Charlotte had been adamant about that.

Now that she was on the spot, the words couldn't come out.

She gave Gina a wobbly smile, trying to summon up her courage to say that crucial word "five," but the elderly woman spoke first.

"I can go no lower than twenty percent less," Gina said firmly.

Olivia nearly fell over.

"What?" she squeaked, unable to believe what she was hearing.

Twenty percent?

She could afford it now, and her cushion of funds would be bigger than the bare minimum that she needed.

"Twenty less. Take it or leave it, it is my final offer," Gina said, sounding firm.

"I would like to accept your very generous offer," Olivia said in a wobbly voice. Thank you so much."

Her head was spinning and she needed to sit down, preferably with a big glass of wine in her hand. She couldn't believe what had just happened.

It was hers now. The farm was hers.

"It is a deal, then," the woman said. "I will send you the payment details later this afternoon. Good luck with the winemaking, signorina. When your first vintage is ready, I will purchase a bottle."

She headed back to the car.

Slowly, the Fiat drove away.

"I don't believe it," Olivia whispered as Charlotte punched the air in delight, causing Erba to caper around the garden, kicking up her heels.

Olivia sat down on the edge of the porch, placing her hands on the warm stone as she looked out over the view. Her view.

She was stunned by how fast her life had transformed. She thought she would end up back where she started, but then, in a dizzying twist, her world had turned topsy-turvy again.

Now she was at the start of a brand new adventure. Even though she had no idea where it might lead, or if her winemaking dream would ever come true, Olivia felt glad she'd finally ignored the advice of her head, and followed her heart.

Now Available for Pre-Order!

AGED FOR DEATH
(A Tuscan Vineyard Cozy Mystery–Book 2)

"Very entertaining. I highly recommend this book to the permanent library of any reader that appreciates a very well written mystery, with some twists and an intelligent plot. You will not be disappointed. Excellent way to spend a cold weekend!"

—Books and Movie Reviews, Roberto Mattos (regarding *Murder in the Manor*)

AGED FOR DEATH (A TUSCAN VINEYARD COZY MYSTERY) is book #2 in a charming new cozy mystery series by #1 bestselling author Fiona Grace, author of Murder in the Manor (Book #1), a #1 Bestseller with over 100 five-star reviews—and a free download!

Olivia Glass, 34, turns her back on her life as a high-powered executive in Chicago and relocates to Tuscany, determined to start a new, simpler life—and to grow her own vineyard.

Olivia is falling in love with the Tuscan life and the gorgeous Tuscan scenery, especially as she travels to visit Pisa. Yet when the winery she works for auctions off a rare and expensive bottle of wine–and when someone turns up dead–Olivia must draw on her strength as a sommelier to get to the bottom of the murder.

In the meanwhile, her new own attempts at a vineyard—and her love life—are failing miserably.

Can Olivia turn it all around to create the life she's always dreamed of? Or was it all a fantasy that she should let go?

Hilarious, packed with travel, food, wine, twists and turns, romance and her newfound animal friend—and centering around a baffling small-town murder that Olivia must solve—AGED FOR DEATH is an un-putdownable cozy that will keep you laughing late into the night.

Book #3 in the series—AGED FOR MAYHEM—is now also available!

AGED FOR DEATH
(A Tuscan Vineyard Cozy Mystery–Book 2)

Made in the USA
Las Vegas, NV
28 September 2022